GHOSTLY DESPAIR

A HARPER HARLOW MYSTERY BOOK TEN

LILY HARPER HART

ONE

"Does thou want to taste my wrath?"

Harper Harlow, her flaxen hair pulled back in a simple ponytail, planted her hands on her hips and glared in the direction she believed the ghost she hunted was hiding. "Knock that off!"

"Who are you talking to?"

Zander Pritchett, Harper's best friend and a co-owner of Ghost Hunters, Inc., tilted his head to the side as he listened for a voice he could never hear. Harper was the talent in their little operation — although Zander would never purposely admit that — and she was the only one who could see and talk to ghosts. Zander provided accounting know-how and enthusiasm ... and the occasional snarky comment.

"Who do you think I'm talking to?" Harper let her agitation out to play as her blue eyes fired with annoyance. "There's only one other person in this theater."

"I don't want to be annoying, but technically there are only two people in this theater," Zander countered. "You ... and me." His finger bounced between them. "Whatever you're talking to isn't a person."

"It's a former person," Harper argued.

"That's not the point. It's not a person now. That's the point."

"I don't understand why we're arguing at all."

His dark hair gleaming under the limited light of the Midnight Express Theater chandelier, Zander made an exaggerated face. "We're arguing because we enjoy it. We communicate best when snark and screaming are involved."

Harper wanted to argue, but it was impossible. "Yes, well, we have to figure out how to handle this ghost." She was determined as she faced off with her longtime best friend. "We need to go shopping for Thanksgiving dinner — you were the one who insisted we cook together — and that means we need to go to the store."

"We have days to shop."

"The grocery store is a madhouse before Thanksgiving. I want to be done today ... so we don't have to go back."

Zander rolled his eyes so hard Harper was surprised he didn't topple over. "There's no way we're going to get everything on the first try. That's not how cooking a gourmet feast works. We're going to have to make at least three trips back to the supermarket ... so brace yourself for that and suck it up."

Harper didn't like his tone. "Says who?"

"Says anyone who has ever cooked Thanksgiving dinner."

Annoyed, Harper ran her tongue over her teeth as the ghost behind the curtain started making moaning noises. "Knock that off!" She extended a warning finger in the ghost's direction. She hadn't yet been able to get a good look at it — just a good listen — but she was fairly certain it was a female. That explained the drama.

"I maintain that we can get everything we need in one shot," Harper supplied after a beat. "That's why we made a list."

"I'm sure we forgot to put something on the list."

"No, I've been over the list several times. We have everything we need."

"Oh, well, if you've been over it." Zander offered her an exaggerated eye roll. "What about the capers?"

Harper wrinkled her nose. "Why would we possibly need capers?"

"Because they enhance the turkey."

"In what universe?"

"The one I'm going to kick you out of if you don't stop being a pain," Zander replied without hesitation. "I need capers."

"Fine." Harper held her hands up in capitulation. "We'll buy capers. We can add that to today's list."

"I'm going to need fresh acorn squash, too." Zander refused to back down. "It's better if we get that fresh."

Harper recognized exactly what he was doing, and she refused to play the game. "We're getting the squash from the farmer's market. It will be fresh and organic that way, two of your favorite things. We won't have to go to the crowded grocery store for that."

Zander scowled. "That's hardly the point."

"That's exactly the point."

The ghost, losing interest with her moaning, floated through the curtain so she could watch the bickering twosome. Overdressed – like a stage star from sixty years before – she was legitimately fascinated with the conversation.

"You're being difficult just to be difficult." Zander shook his head and made a show of silently cursing so Harper could know what he was saying without actually having to utter the words. "You're ruining my Thanksgiving buzz, Harp. You know how I feel about Thanksgiving."

"I do know how you feel about Thanksgiving," Harper confirmed, softening. "It's one of your favorite holidays, after Halloween, Christmas, and Mardi Gras."

"It is," Zander agreed. "That's why I volunteered to host dinner this year."

Harper harbored suspicions that Zander volunteered to host because he was a control freak who wanted to be in charge of every aspect of the holiday — including decorations and cooking — but she kept that theory to herself. "I'm fine with you hosting dinner."

"It will be the last dinner we have together," Zander reminded her. "You'll be in your own place by Christmas."

Ah, there it is. Harper had been wondering why Zander was being such a pill, but now she understood. He was feeling sorry for himself because they were no longer going to be roommates. She was moving in with her boyfriend Jared Monroe, and Zander's boyfriend Shawn Donovan was taking her place in the house she currently shared with her best friend. Even though he made a big show of being supportive, Zander vacillated wildly whenever the subject of Harper moving popped up and the effervescent blonde suspected he was about to panic.

"I will be in my own place for Christmas," Harper agreed, choosing her words carefully. "I guess it's good that my new place and your place are directly across the road from each other, huh? We counted. It's like fifty footsteps from your front door to mine. That's not bad."

"It's not good." Zander folded his arms across his chest and glared at the curtain when it started moving. He couldn't see the ghost, but that didn't mean he didn't recognize shenanigans when they were about to make an appearance. "Knock that off!"

Harper swallowed a laugh at her best friend's serious expression.

"Now, where were we?" Zander smoothed the front of his tan polo shirt. He was a big fan of dressing for the season. That meant muted browns and oranges for Thanksgiving and festive reds and greens for Christmas. Once Easter rolled around, he would spend two months boasting pastels that made most men cringe.

"You were about to tell me why fifty footsteps is too far for us to be apart," Harper replied.

"Right. We're going into the winter season. You know what that means, right?"

Harper bobbed her head. "Hot chocolate, skiing, ice skating, and snowmobiles."

Zander shot her a withering look. "That means snow, ice, broken bones, and blizzards. That's on top of sub-zero temperatures."

"I thought you liked winter because the clothes are so cute."

"I'm a big fan of the clothes. Boots and scarves need to be modified for summer because they're so freaking awesome. That will never change. However, I am not a fan of the way our road ices. What's going to happen if we get freezing rain? That turns the roads treacherous, so crossing will be akin to risking our lives. We won't be able to see each other."

Harper barely contained her eye roll. "Somehow I think we'll manage."

"Yeah? Well, I don't."

Zander was firm. "I think you should wait until after the snow is finished for the season to move. It will be safer for everyone involved."

"So, basically you're saying you want me to stay with you until February, huh?"

"March," Zander corrected automatically. "We still get snow in March ... and sometimes April. Yeah, April will be better now that I really give it some thought."

Harper bit back a sigh, reminding herself that Zander didn't mean to be a pain. He merely said the things he said out of love. "Zander?"

"Yes, Harp?"

"I'm still going to move, but I promise we'll spend as much time together as we already do even after I move in with Jared. Nothing is going to change. It's just ... my bedroom is going to be a little farther away now."

"Maybe I don't want your bedroom to be farther away. Have you ever considered that?"

"You're going to be fine."

"Oh, well, if you say it then it must be true." Zander adopted a petulant pout as he jutted his lower lip out. "I don't think I'll ever get over this betrayal."

Harper slid her eyes to the curious ghost who hovered two feet away. "You're lucky. You don't have to deal with things like this because you're dead."

The ghost snickered, her laughter delightfully young and hearty. "And people said I was dramatic in life."

"He has a way about him," Harper agreed. "On a different note, though, do you want to go over to the other side? They're sick of you here, but I'm betting there's community theater if you're willing to cross over. That seems right up your alley."

The ghost was clearly intrigued. "Tell me more."

. . .

JARED MONROE CHECKED his text messages before exiting the police cruiser his partner Mel Kelsey pulled to the side along County Line Road.

"What are you looking at?" Mel asked, his tone laced with impatience. "If you and Harper are playing that dirty text game again, I'm going to report you for abusing official department property."

"Ha, ha," Jared sneered, clutching his coat tighter as the wind hit him. "Man, it feels like snow."

"Not yet," Mel countered. "It's a little too early in the season for that. Soon, though. I'm sure we'll have a day or two of nice weather before it happens."

"This is a lot colder than I remember it being on the other side of the state," Jared complained.

"Did you live on the lake on the west side?"

"Close enough."

"But did you live right on the lake?" Mel persisted. "That's the difference here. In the summer, the lake offers a comfortable breeze that makes Whisper Cove a lovely vacation destination. In the winter, that same lake makes this a place where snow piles high and the cold is overbearing."

"How do you live with it?"

"Hot chocolate and warm fires. I believe you have a fireplace in your new house, right? Things should be fine."

Jared brightened at mention of his new home. "Yeah. Maybe I should place a call and order some wood. We're probably going to need that, right?"

"If you want to stay warm this winter."

"I'll call after work." Jared put a notation in his phone calendar before checking his messages a second time. He knew his phone would've dinged if Harper texted, like she promised, but he couldn't stop himself from hoping that he somehow missed her update.

"What's your problem?" Mel asked, reading his partner perfectly. "Why do you keep looking at your phone?"

"Harper and Zander are on a job."

"So? That's good. That means they'll bring money in during the holiday season. Since I have a feeling you and Harper will go over-board for Christmas — I know you will because Harper and Zander already go overboard and you're a schmuck where your girlfriend is concerned — the money will come in handy."

"I don't care about that," Jared countered. "She was supposed to message when she was done, though, and I'm worried. She said it would be a quick job, and they've been at it for at least two hours."

"You could always text her," Mel pointed out.

"I don't want her to think I'm checking up on her."

"But that's what you want to do."

"Kind of," Jared hedged, sheepish. "I just want to know she's safe. Sue me."

Mel chuckled, genuinely amused. Jared hadn't yet been in town a full year, but he was getting used to his partner's moods and attitude. Watching Jared fall in love with Harper had been a genuine delight. Since Mel had known the girl since she was a small child — he was Zander's uncle, after all, so he had a first-row seat to watch their hijinks over the years — he was happy to play witness to a real-life love story. Unfortunately for him, that love sometimes took on a fervent tone.

"She's fine. She's been taking care of herself for a very long time."

"I know that."

"If you know that, why are you obsessing about her? For all you know, she simply could've forgotten to text. She's probably having pumpkin coffee with Zander and laughing about whatever goofy thing their ghost did. Don't have a conniption fit — especially when you have no reason to do it."

"Thanks. I'll keep that in mind." Jared pocketed his phone and turned his attention to the scene in front of him. "So, what are we doing out here again?"

"Accident," Mel replied grimly.

"I figured that out myself when I saw the car in the ditch. It looks as if emergency personnel are already out here, though. With only one vehicle, do they really need us on the scene?"

"The car rolled," Mel explained. "We have to take measurements.

The way it is, the driver was already lucky. This bend is sharp, and a lot of cars end up in the water over yonder once the weather turns bad and the roads icy."

Jared followed Mel's gaze to the lake. In the summer, it was a beautiful place to enjoy lazy weekends while reading a magazine and hanging with his girlfriend. Now, with the trees bare and the wind biting, there was something stark about the view. "I take it to mean you've had a lot of accidents out here."

"We have," Mel confirmed, scratching his cheek as he inclined his chin. "In fact, this is the area where Quinn Jackson went missing. His car was found in almost the exact same spot, but we never found him ... or his body."

Jared slowed his pace, his stomach twisting at the words. He recognized the name. Quinn Jackson was long before his time, but he occasionally felt as if he knew the man because he'd been dating Harper at the time of his disappearance. When Jared first hooked up with Harper, he worried she was still mourning the man she loved. Very quickly, he realized that Harper never loved Quinn. She cared about him, felt guilty because she couldn't track down his ghost and offer relief, but she didn't love him. That's what she told Jared anyway.

He had no reason to mistrust her, Jared reminded himself as a shiver ran down his spine. She'd never been anything but completely and totally honest with him. That's one of the reasons he was initially leery about dating her. She hunted ghosts, for crying out loud, and she was proud of it.

Chemistry is a funny thing, though, and Jared found he couldn't stay away from her. He was head-over-heels in love in what felt like the blink of an eye, and he had no intention of looking back. He was happy, they were moving forward. Still, Quinn Jackson was one of those figures who hid in the shadows and intermittently popped up at the exact moment Jared didn't want to think about him. He would probably never be completely out of their lives.

"This is the spot, huh?" Jared took a long beat to look over the rough terrain in every direction. "I can see why he would've gone over the road here, but not why you couldn't find his body. A lot of this space is open."

"Except there's a big expanse of open area that way." Mel pointed for emphasis. "The assumption was he sustained injuries in the accident. A lot of blood was found on the car door. His path led in that direction before disappearing.

"The medical examiner theorized that he had a head injury of some sort and was confused," he continued. "Had he stayed here, we would've found him. He was probably trying to get help, though, and instead he walked to his death."

"So, you believe he's still out there somewhere?"

Mel shrugged. "Where else would he be? We may never find his body because it's been so long. It's sad but ... what can you do?"

"Nothing, I guess." Jared turned his full attention to the shaken woman sitting on the back of the ambulance. A female paramedic with sympathetic eyes busily checked over the trembling woman for injuries, but it was clear the mental toll the accident took on the driver was worse than the physical toll. "How are you feeling?"

"Fine." The woman offered a wan smile. "I'm ... fine. I guess you could say that I'm lucky."

"I'll say so." Mel's smile was much more gregarious than that of his partner. He was good at putting victims at ease, and his world-famous charm was on full display now. "Can you tell us what happened?"

Her name was Vicky Thompson and she was a St. Clair County resident. She said she was familiar with the road and wasn't speeding, but a deer bolting over the highway caused her to react out of instinct and overcorrect to avoid the animal. The next thing she knew, she was upside down in the ditch ... and freaking out.

"I didn't think I could even get out of the car until that man came from nowhere to help me," Vicky explained, rubbing her hands together. "He pulled me out of the window once he was sure I wasn't too badly injured. I would still be in there crying if it wasn't for him."

Mel and Jared exchanged a curious look before turning their attention to the road.

"What man?" Jared asked finally. "Was he a passerby?"

Vicky shrugged, noncommittal. "He would have to be, right? What else would he be doing out here?"

"But where did he go?" Mel pressed. "I mean ... why did he leave? Did he give a reason for not waiting to talk to us?"

"He didn't really speak." Vicky was blasé. "He helped me out of the car, made sure I was all right, helped me dial 911, and then he took off."

"Wait." Jared held up his hand to still her. "Are you saying that he didn't call for help?"

"No. I did."

"What about a vehicle?" Mel asked. "You must have seen a vehicle."

"I don't know." Vicky's eyes flashed. "I don't remember much. I was shaken. I'd just been in an accident, for crying out loud. Still ... he must've had a car. How else would he have gotten out here?"

"How else indeed," Jared muttered under his breath as he turned his attention to the tire marks across the way. "That's weird, right?"

Mel nodded. "Definitely. It's not technically against the law, though."

"Leaving the scene of an accident is against the law."

"He stopped to help and then left. He had nothing to do with the accident so ... that's not breaking the law."

Jared disagreed, but it was hardly his biggest worry. "We should see if we can find tire treads. You know ... just in case."

"Just in case of what?"

The younger police officer didn't have an answer. All he knew was that he was uncomfortable with the turn of events. "Let's just cover our bases, huh? We'll go by the book."

"Fine. That sounds like a plan to me."

TWO

Harper and Zander were knee deep in an argument when Jared let himself into the house shortly after his shift. He could hear them from the driveway, which didn't bode well for the relaxing evening he had planned.

"What seems to be the problem, kids?" He shed his coat and left it on the rack before moving to the couch and giving Harper a welcoming kiss. "How come you didn't text when you were done with your job?"

Flustered by the argument and conversational shift, Harper furrowed her brow. "I thought I did."

"You didn't."

"Oh, well, I'm sorry."

She looked appropriately chastised, so Jared decided to let it go. "I was worried, but you look as if you're in one piece."

"She was a perfectly lovely ghost. She didn't put up much of a fight. Er, well, after the initial moaning and groaning."

"It was an easy job," Zander volunteered, a cookbook open on his lap. "Harper is the one being a pain in the butt."

"I am not." Harper's eyes fired, causing Jared to smirk as he sank onto the couch and collected her hand. "You're the one being a pain."

"I am sunshine and joy, and you know it!"

"Oh, whatever." Harper looked to be at the end of her rope, something Jared recognized after months of sharing space with the rambunctious friends. "You're the one who suggested I put off my move until after the snow flies because freezing rain might make it so we never see each other again."

Zander bristled at her dismissive tone. "That's a legitimate concern."

Jared bit back a sigh. While Harper and Zander were never quiet — like ... never — the arguments that had popped up since news of shifting living arrangements became everyday household conversations were something to behold. "I'm sure she'll be okay. If you're that worried, I'll buy extra ice melt to make sure her treks between houses are safe. Trust me. I'm the last person who wants Harper to suffer from a broken bone."

"Ice melt?" Zander turned haughty. "Do you have any idea how bad ice melt is for the environment?"

"Honestly? No."

"Well, it's not good. It's killed animals ... and plants ... and people. Harper is better staying here until April."

Jared merely shook his head. "No. You're simply getting cold feet. This is all going to work out for the best. Tell me what you guys were arguing about ... unless it was about Harper not moving. I cannot listen to that fight one more time."

Harper's smile was rueful. "You know you're going to have to listen to that argument at least another twenty times, right? It's not simply going to go away because you want it to."

"You don't know. The power of positive thinking and all that. If I put it out there into the universe, it might come back and benefit me threefold."

"You've been watching too much television," Zander chided. "I'm never going to let it go."

"I know." Jared rubbed his forehead and focused on the cookbook. "Are you guys arguing over dinner or something?"

"Not dinner tonight," Zander replied. "Shawn is picking up subs, by the way. He should be home in a few minutes."

"That sounds good."

"We're arguing about Thanksgiving dinner," Zander explained. "I'm going to cook it and Harper is going to eat and love it ... if she ever shuts her hole."

Harper's eye roll was so pronounced it caused Jared's heart to fill with warmth. The expressiveness of her face was one of his favorite things about her.

"Are you anti-Thanksgiving dinner and nobody told me about it?" Jared teased, poking her side. "I don't know if we can continue if you don't love mashed potatoes and turkey."

"I'm fine with mashed potatoes and turkey," Harper said. "I'm not fine with Zander's insistence on taking over everything. We were supposed to be doing this together. You know, a last hurrah before we split into different houses. He's being bossy, though, and I'm sick of it."

"Ah. I see." And, because he did see, Jared settled in for what he was sure would be a bitter stretch of days. He knew why Zander was picking a fight. The man couldn't deal with his emotions — he was legitimately sad about Harper moving out — and the field he chose to wage his battle on was the Thanksgiving dinner table.

For her part, Harper was only arguing back because she was nervous. The idea of living away from Zander, even only across the road, made her antsy. Jared recognized this, found her reaction mildly cute, and decided to participate in the argument.

"So, what's the problem?" He asked before the sniping could recommence. "Is there an argument about deep-fried turkey versus pan-roasted turkey? If so, I don't care either way as long as there is turkey."

The look on Zander's face, the horrified bafflement, told Jared he'd taken a misstep. "What did I say?" He looked to Harper for help. "I was trying to be a peacemaker."

Harper chuckled as she patted his leg. "You couldn't possibly realize that Zander thinks deep-fried turkey is an abomination."

"If turkey was meant to be deep-fried, there would be more things made out of turkey on sticks," Zander barked. "Turkey is meant to be rubbed with garlic and herbs, loved, and delicately roasted at the perfect temperature over hours to trap in moisture. It is not meant to be lowered into a vat of bubbling oil for thirty minutes."

Jared recognized right away that he'd stepped in it. "I take it back. Roasting turkey is the only way to go."

Harper smirked at her boyfriend's discomfort. "We actually agree on the turkey. What we don't agree on is the sides."

"Stuffing, mashed potatoes and gravy, rolls. That's all I need," Jared offered.

Zander's scowl was back. "That's the Neanderthal way of celebrating Thanksgiving."

"I don't think Thanksgiving was around when the Neanderthals were," Jared offered helpfully. "Besides, since they were focused on fire and using rocks as tools, I'm pretty sure they would've taken their turkey any way they could get it."

Zander's expression was withering. "Oh, you're so witty."

Despite himself, Jared chuckled. "I am. I thought about being a standup comedian — or a clown — when I was a kid. Ultimately, being a police officer won out. The lure of clown college still calls to me."

Harper pressed her lips together to keep from laughing. Jared was a master when it came to messing with Zander. He knew exactly what to say to drive her best friend batty.

"You would make a lovely clown," Zander said dryly. "I honestly think you should've gone that route. Harper would've never moved in with you then. She's terrified of clowns."

Harper balked. "I'm not terrified."

Jared's grin was lazy as he slid it to her. "I didn't know you had coulrophobia."

"I don't know what that is."

"Fear of clowns."

"I can't believe you know that word," Harper marveled. "I didn't know that was a real thing."

"They have a phobia for everything." Zander waved his hand dismissively. "To be fair, though, clowns are creepy. I don't like them either. Sure, I would protect Harper if a killer clown attacked, but otherwise, I would like to avoid them."

"Me, too." Harper involuntarily shuddered as she shifted closer to Jared. "Don't ever dress up like a clown, by the way. You'll be sleeping alone for weeks until I can get the memory of that white makeup out of my head."

"Duly noted." Jared pressed an absent kiss to Harper's forehead before shifting his eyes to the opening door.

Shawn, his arms laden with subs and bags of fries, grinned when he saw everyone grouped together. "This looks nice. No arguing tonight?"

"Oh, they've been arguing," Jared countered. "Right now they're fighting over sides for Thanksgiving dinner."

"Fun." Shawn delivered the subs and fries to the coffee table. "Speaking of Thanksgiving, my mother is not coming. She says she will be here for Christmas if she can manage, but she's trying to spread her time between my siblings and me, and she doesn't want to visit until we're officially living together so she can cast aspersions on our decorating choices."

Zander's expression turned imperious. "No one can cast aspersions on my decorating choices. My taste is impeccable. That's why Harper and Jared are going to let me serve as an interior designer at their place."

Now it was Jared's turn to snort. "Over my dead body."

"That can be arranged."

"Let's not argue about this again," Harper suggested, holding up her hands to dissuade her boyfriend and best friend from throwing down. "Let's go back to talk about sides. Although, you said your mother might be coming for Thanksgiving, Jared. Is she?"

"She's not," Jared replied, choking back a smirk at the relieved look on Harper's face. She picked the oddest times to be nervous, and Jared was amused she seemed legitimately worried about meeting his mother. "She is, however, coming for Christmas."

Harper's eyelids fluttered. "She is?"

"Yup. She wants to see the new house, too, but she wants to wait until we're actually moved in. She's spending Thanksgiving with my sister and Christmas with us."

"Oh." Harper's cheeks burned as she absorbed the words. "That means we're going to need to get a guest room ready." She scratched her cheek, her mind working at a fantastic rate. "We don't even have a bed for the guest room."

"Chill out, drama queen." Jared gave her hand a firm squeeze as he fought the urge to laugh. Harper very rarely appeared flustered. She was a strong and confident woman, which was one of the things that first drew him to her ... other than her looks, of course, but he didn't want to be shallow and focus on that. She was positively apoplectic now. "My mother is one of the easiest people in the world to get along with. I've told her all about you. She's already as in love as I am."

Harper nodded absently. "Right. We're going to need sheets ... and towels for the guest bathroom ... and I'm sure we're going to need fifty other things."

"Don't worry about that, Harp," Zander admonished as he unwrapped his sub. "We can fix that together. We have plenty of time. We need to focus on Thanksgiving before we worry about Christmas. Both of your parents are coming for dinner, right?"

Harper crashed back to the here and now. "Yes." Her dislike of the conversational shift was obvious. "My mother claims she's bringing a date, which means my father will probably bring a date, too."

Shawn's forehead wrinkled. "I thought they were divorced."

"It's a never-ending process," Zander explained. "They spent more than twenty years fighting to the point where Harper dreaded they would get a divorce only to wait until she was an adult to spring it on her. The divorce has been ongoing for years, though. They're fighting over every little thing in the property dispute ... including those black tulip bulbs your mother picked up from the Netherlands, right?"

Harper nodded, her face going slack. "Yes. There's an odd number of bulbs somehow, even though they both swear up and down there were twelve when they bought them. They're both convinced that someone stole the missing bulb."

"Don't animals eat those things?" Jared asked, taking the time to unwrap Harper's sub for her to make sure she ate.

"That's what I said, but they're convinced it was stolen and now they're going to mediation over the bulb. They're never going to get divorced at this rate."

"Maybe that's the point," Shawn suggested, taking everyone by surprise. "Maybe they don't really want to get divorced so they're putting on a big show to drag things out."

"That would be nice, but I don't think so," Harper said. "They're far too interested in making each other miserable than harboring feelings of love for one another. They're just ... weird people."

"I think they're fun," Zander countered. "Dinner will be fine. Your parents will serve as the entertainment."

Harper wasn't happy at the prospect. "Maybe we should lock them out of the house or something."

"We'll save that as a last resort." Zander was all business as he turned back to the cookbook. "By the way, Jared, you're not allergic to anything, are you? I talked to Uncle Mel this afternoon, and he reminded me that he's allergic to sage. I want to make sure I don't accidentally kill anyone."

"I don't have any food allergies," Jared confirmed. "When did you talk to Mel?"

"Um ... I think you guys were at the hospital. That's what he told me anyway. Why?"

"Because, he didn't tell me he talked to you," Jared complained. "If he had, I would've known you and Harper were fine and I wouldn't have worried."

"You don't have to worry," Harper reminded him as she popped a fry into her mouth. "I can take care of myself. I know what I'm doing."

"Love makes it impossible for me not to worry." Jared kissed the tip of her nose. "I'm a slave to my feelings for you. I can't change it, so you're going to have to live with it."

"Fair enough." Harper swallowed her fry. "Why were you at the hospital, by the way? You didn't get hurt, did you?"

"No. There was an accident out on County Line Road, not far from the water. A woman rolled her car and was injured. She seemed fine on the scene, but the paramedics insisted on transporting her to the hospital just to be on the safe side. We had a few follow-up questions after the initial consult, so we talked to her there."

"Is she okay?"

"She seems fine. A little banged up, but nothing to get worked up about. Mel says that's a dangerous road. It's right where Quinn Jackson was killed." Jared realized his mistake too late to take it back. He hadn't meant to bring up the man's death so cavalierly. "I mean ... I'm sorry."

Harper's face drained of color before she collected herself. "It's fine," she said after a beat. "It was a long time ago."

"What was a long time ago?" Shawn asked, curious.

"Harper's former boyfriend died on that road," Zander replied, his gaze heavy and his voice low. "They never found his body, just his vehicle. It was a bad accident. It was assumed he wandered into the woods and succumbed to his injuries, although we can't be sure."

"That's awful." Shawn looked to Jared, sympathy positively rolling off him. "I can't imagine dealing with something like that. Is there no way to search the woods?"

Jared cleared his throat, uncomfortable. "It's been a long time, years. Mel told me that dogs were sent into the woods, but they never found a trace of him. It's unusual but not unheard of. At this point in time, well, finding him would be a fluke. There wouldn't be much left of his body."

"Oh." Realization dawned on Shawn. "That's ... awful."

"It is," Harper agreed, abandoning her sub on the table and standing. "It was a tragedy. I looked for his ghost but never found it. I'll always be sorry that I couldn't lay him to rest."

"Where are you going?" Jared asked gently. "Aren't you hungry?"

"Not really. I think I'm going to take a bath." Harper averted her eyes. "You guys can split my sub between you."

Jared opened his mouth to argue, but Zander gave him an almost imperceptible shake of his head, forcing him to change course. "Okay. I'll stay out here and finish my dinner. You should relax for as long as you want in the tub."

Harper forced a smile that didn't make it all the way to her eyes. "That's the plan."

Jared waited until Harper disappeared into the bedroom to speak again. "What was that?"

"Don't get worked up about it," Zander supplied. "She never wants to talk about him. I told you before, it's not because he was the love of her life. It's the guilt she feels because he wasn't that fuels her."

"I think it's more than that," Jared persisted. "She was clearly upset when I mentioned another accident happening in the same spot."

"She was upset because she thinks she failed Quinn," Zander countered. "You have to understand, she pictures him out there wandering around the woods looking for someone to help him cross over."

"Is that a possibility?" Shawn queried.

Zander shrugged. "I guess, in theory, it could be like that. It's far more likely that Quinn slipped away and his soul passed over on its own. Remember, ghosts are the exception. Not everyone comes back as a ghost."

"Why would she assume that Quinn is a ghost?" Shawn asked.

"Because, in the hours after the accident, she wanted to be proactive," Jared said. "She originally thought he was out there suffering, right? The medical examiner said there was too much blood at the scene for anybody to survive. She imagined a terrible death, and finding his ghost is the only way to alleviate the weight she feels pressing her down where his death is concerned."

"That's basically it in a nutshell," Zander agreed. "Harper cared about Quinn. She's too good of a person to ever date someone without feeling something. She didn't love him, though. I think, especially now that she knows what real love is, she feels guilty. Quinn only stayed in the area because of her."

"Oh, so she thinks that if she let him go, he would probably still be alive," Shawn surmised. "She can't take that on herself. It's not her fault. It was an accident."

"Tell her that," Jared said ruefully. "She can't completely let it go. I shouldn't have brought up the accident."

"She'll be fine," Zander promised. "A good night's sleep will make everything better."

Jared could only hope that was true.

THREE

Harper woke with a smile, which allowed some of the worry squeezing Jared's heart to ease. He cuddled her close the moment her eyes popped open and pressed a kiss to her forehead.

"How did you sleep?"

"I slept fine. How did you sleep?"

In truth, Jared's slumber had been more restless. He woke at least five times, checking on Harper to make sure she wasn't awake and fretting each time he shifted. "Good. I could hear the wind outside, though. I think it's going to be another cold day."

"You should get used to that."

"I miss hammocking."

Harper broke out into a wide grin. Before this past summer, Jared had never been in a hammock. Once introduced to the joys of a lazy day by the water, book in hand, he was almost impossible to drag from the hammock.

"May will eventually wind its way around. Until then, we can go snowshoeing and skiing."

Jared made a face. "That doesn't sound nearly as much fun as laying around with you in nothing but a skimpy bathing suit. You're going to be buried in snow pants and coats for winter events."

"True, but just think how much fun it will be to shed the winter clothes and snuggle together under a blanket by the fire."

"Good point." Jared gave her another kiss before stretching, his eyes drifting to the window. "We should start taking loads of clothes to the house. In fact, I've been packing stuff at my rental and I'm almost completely done. I want to get out of there so Jeff can take over the space."

"How many loads do you think you have?"

"Only two. None of the furniture there is mine."

"Well, then let's pick a day over the weekend to drive out there," Harper suggested. "Between your truck and my car, we should be able to handle everything. I'm sure we can con Zander and Shawn into helping us carry the boxes, too."

Jared cocked a dubious eyebrow. "Zander?"

Harper shrugged. "Well, Shawn at least. He'll probably be able to guilt Zander into helping. If that doesn't work, we'll gush about how strong Shawn is and Zander won't be able to stop himself from competing."

"That sounds like a plan." Jared lazily trailed his finger up and down Harper's spine. He wanted to question her about her reaction the previous evening, but he was convinced it was a poor idea. Still, he couldn't shake the inclination. "About last night ... ."

"What about it?"

"I'm sorry if I said something to make you uncomfortable." Jared ran his hand down the back of Harper's hair to smooth it. She wasn't a fan of her bedhead, but he couldn't get enough of it. She looked adorable upon waking. Of course, Jared thought pretty much everything she did was adorable. "I didn't mean to upset you."

Harper rubbed between her eyebrows as she regarded him. "I know. I shouldn't have reacted the way I did. It's just ... I don't like thinking about it. It makes me sick to my stomach."

"Heart, I get that. I wish you would talk to me, though."

"I don't know what there is to say." Harper propped herself on an elbow and pressed her hand to his chiseled chest. "He's gone. He's been gone a long time. He was gone long before you entered my life. I don't want you worrying about him."

"I'm not worried about him," Jared clarified. "I'm worried about what you feel for him. Wait, that came out wrong. It makes me sound jealous. I don't feel jealous." That was mostly true. In his darkest moments, something he would never admit to anyone, he occasionally felt a twinge of jealousy regarding Quinn.

It would've been better, he theorized, if Quinn hadn't died and he could've made a clean break with Harper. The death notwithstanding, which obviously weighed on her heavily, it was the guilt that fueled her most. She blamed herself for much of what happened, and Jared couldn't help but wonder if that would be different had the relationship been allowed to come to its natural end.

"I know you're not jealous." Harper's smile was easy and heartfelt. "Just for the record, though, you have nothing to feel jealous about. I love you ... completely."

"I love you, too." Jared cupped the back of her head. "You have no idea how much I love you."

"I think I do. I feel the same way about you."

"Still, I shouldn't have brought up Quinn's death," Jared persisted. "I didn't realize it would upset you the way it did. I'm sorry."

"Don't apologize."

"I'm still sorry."

A smile, unbidden, curved Harper's lips. "You're even cute when you're apologizing for no reason."

"I have a way about me," Jared agreed.

"I wasn't upset because you brought up Quinn," Harper clarified. "I simply don't like to talk about it because it gives me nightmares."

"It does?"

"I dream about what it must have been like for him; to be hurt, dying, and trying to find help. In my dreams, I can feel the blood pouring out of me as I struggle to stay on my feet. It used to be that I was searching for Zander in my dreams, because I needed help and he always wants to help. Don't tell him, but that shifted to you several months back.

"I'm always looking for you, bleeding out, and I know I'm going to die," she continued. "I'm desperate to find you so I can tell you I love you one last time, be with you when I go instead of alone. I think that's what bothers me most, that he was alone."

"Oh, Heart." Jared dragged her onto his chest and tightened his arms around her back as he pressed his cheek to her forehead. "I think that dying alone could be one of the worst possible things. Although, dying in your sleep sounds like the easiest. If you know you're dying, though, being alone has to be the most terrifying thing imaginable."

"Yeah."

"The thing is, and I don't know a lot about the case because obviously I wasn't here, but if Quinn was severely injured he was probably dazed and numb," Jared offered. "Most likely, he didn't know what was happening. It would've been like going to sleep."

"I hope that's true. The idea of him suffering makes me feel sick."

"I know. You have a good heart." Jared took them both by surprise when he switched positions and rolled so Harper was under him, causing her to giggle. "Now, I was thinking, perhaps we can go overboard on togetherness to make both of us feel better about these deep thoughts neither of us wants to dwell on before breakfast. How does that sound?"

"Like the best offer I've had all day."

"That's what I was going for."

JARED NEVER GOT TO eat breakfast with his makeshift family. A phone call from Mel — one telling him that Vicky Thompson had a setback — forced him to drag on clothes and leave the house with wet hair.

He met his partner at the hospital lobby and asked the obvious question rather than utter a friendly greeting.

"What happened?"

Mel held his hands palms out and shrugged. "I just got here myself. Daniel Steele — don't make romance books jokes, whatever you do — called first thing this morning and insisted I get out here. He said he needed to talk about Vicky Thompson. I assumed there was something wrong — like maybe she remembered something — but all he would tell me was that she died in the night."

All the oxygen whooshed out of Jared's lungs. "What? She died? But ... how? I mean, she was a little banged up after the accident and emotionally worked up, but she didn't suffer any life-threatening injuries."

"You know as much as I do," Mel said. "We're supposed to meet Daniel in his office." Mel led the way to the secretary station at the center of the lobby. "We're here to see Daniel Steele. He's expecting us."

"Certainly, sir." The nurse, whose name tag read "Kimberly," gave Jared a shy smile as she pressed a button on her phone. "Are you here together?"

"We're not a couple or anything, if that's what you're asking," Mel said dryly. "We're both going to the same meeting, though."

Jared pursed his lips at his partner's dark expression. "What?"

"You have a strange effect on women. They all go weak at the knees and giggly whenever you're around. It's annoying."

"I have the same effect on certain men, too," Jared offered, smirking. "Just ask your nephew."

"Oh, please." Mel rolled his eyes. "You're not Zander's type. He would've dumped you right away because of the over-sized nipples thing. You wouldn't have made it to a second date with my nephew."

Jared widened his eyes to comical proportions. "I don't have over-sized nipples."

"That's not what Zander says."

"Yeah, well, he's a freak."

"You're just figuring that out?" Mel inclined his chin when a man appeared at the security door and motioned for them to enter the isolated clerical wing of the hospital. Jared fell into step with his partner and allowed Mel to do the talking since he clearly knew the man in charge. "Daniel, this is my partner, Jared Monroe. Jared, this is Daniel. He's the hospital chief."

"It's nice to meet you," Jared offered.

"You, too." Daniel led the two men to his office, firmly shutting the door before taking a seat behind the rich mahogany desk arranged at the center of the room. "You're the man dating Harper Harlow, correct?"

Jared nodded, immediately on edge. "I am. We're moving in together."

"She's a nice girl. I golf with her father. He's a bit of a crazy man. Harper is lucky to be sane given how Phil acts."

"Her mother isn't much better," Mel noted. "Harper is an absolute joy, though. She always has been."

Jared narrowed his eyes. "You call her a pain all the time."

"She is a pain, at least from my perspective," Mel countered. "That doesn't mean I don't love her. I've known her longer than you."

"Whatever." Jared pushed whatever argument he planned to engage Mel in out of his mind, at least until after they were finished at the hospital. "So, Vicky Thompson died? Do you have any idea how?"

"That's what I want to talk to you about." Steele steepled his fingers and rested his elbows on the desk. "Ms. Thompson was brought in after a rollover accident on County Line Road."

"We know, Daniel," Mel said dryly. "We were there."

"I'm sorry. It's just ... this whole thing has taken me by surprise." He mopped his forehead with a handkerchief. "Her initial injuries were mild. She had a bruised rib, several bumps and contusions, and she seemed mildly confused. We thought she might have a concussion, so we ran a few scans, but they came up empty."

"Did you release her?" Mel asked.

Steele shook his head. "Just to be on the safe side, we decided to keep her for observation. I pulled her file myself. She was resting comfortably and watching television. She didn't have any visitors, although she placed a call on her cell phone. That's it."

"I'm not sure why you're telling me this," Mel hedged, confused. "Is there something you're leaving out?"

"At some point in the night, she coded," Steele volunteered. "Our crash team went in, treated her, but couldn't bring her back."

"That means you need to conduct an autopsy, right?" Jared queried.

"That's ongoing right now, but I don't think it will be necessary," Steele said. "While in the room, one of the nurses noticed a slight discoloration in the IV bag next to Ms. Thompson's bed. It was blue when it should've been clear."

"I don't know what that means."

"It means someone injected something into the bag," Steele replied. "We're not sure what, but the substance looks to be caustic. We're running tests, but whatever it was, Ms. Thompson succumbed relatively quickly."

"Wait." Mel shifted on his chair, confused. "Are you saying that she was poisoned?"

"Until we have the test results back, I can't say that with complete certainty," Steele cautioned. "If I were a betting man, though, I would wager on cyanide to be the answer when we get the report back."

Jared was dumbfounded. "Cyanide. But ... how?"

"We don't know. No one registered to see her, and as far as we know, she didn't receive visitors. Ms. Thompson was alone in her room for the duration of the evening, at least as far as we can tell."

Jared's busy brain kicked into overdrive. "Could someone have injected the poison into the IV bag? I mean ... like a nurse or something."

"I guess that's a possibility, but why?" Steele challenged. "What would the motive be?"

"Maybe you have one of those angel-of-death nurses, or a doctor, on your staff," Mel suggested.

"I believe an angel of death believes he or she — and it's often a she — is helping those in pain," Steele explained. "Killing them is an act of mercy, whether real or imagined. Ms. Thompson wasn't in any pain. Sure, she was keyed up from the accident, but her injuries were minor. She should've made a full recovery. She certainly wasn't uncomfortable due to pain."

"So there has to be a reason to kill her," Jared mused, rubbing his chin. "Maybe the rollover wasn't really an accident."

"She said she lost control of her vehicle," Mel argued. "She said she overcorrected because she saw a deer and that caused the car to roll over. I've seen it before in that area, and deer are prevalent."

"For the record, I talked to the duty nurse assigned to Ms. Thompson's floor," Steele said. "She said she didn't spend a lot of time talking to her, but the deer story was repeated multiple times. Ms. Thompson was apparently very upset because she totaled her car."

"Okay, so the accident itself was an accident." Mel's foot busily tapped on the ground. "I don't understand why anyone would track her to the hospital and try to kill her."

"We're running tests on the entire staff," Steele offered. "If anyone tests positive for cyanide on his or her hands, they'll be pulled in for further testing. I'm not confident it was a member of my staff, though. It could've been someone from the outside."

"Do you have cameras here?" Jared asked.

"We do. Security is going over them now."

"We're going to need to look at them, too," Mel pressed. "We need to see who came in and out of the hospital."

"That's fine, but keep in mind, the cameras are pointed at the front and back doors. Only the exits. Oh, and the mental ward up on four because we've had too many lawsuits to risk not having cameras up there. No other area is covered, though."

"Oh." Jared deflated a bit. "May I ask how come?"

"They're unnecessary. We rarely have issues."

"You have one now."

"Yes, and I can promise you that I'm as upset as you are," Steele stressed. "If you think I want news spreading that a woman was poisoned in my hospital, you're wrong. I did my duty, though. I reported the event to you and now I'm waiting to see how you're going to respond."

"What is that supposed to mean?"

"He wants to know if we're going to make the death public," Mel surmised, making a tsking sound with his tongue as he shook his head. "He's worried what will happen if the murder becomes public knowledge."

"I would appreciate discretion," Steele agreed. "If it turns out that a member of my staff is the guilty party, I understand that you will have no choice but to go public. Until you have answers, though, I would prefer things remain on the down low. Theorizing and gossiping aren't going to help anyone."

"I don't disagree with that," Mel said. "The thing is, I can't guarantee anything. Not until I know more, at least. We need to look at the cameras and see the report on the substance found in the IV bag. As of right now, poisoning as a cause of death is still a theory."

"Yes, there is always the possibility that Ms. Thompson succumbed to an injury we weren't aware of," Steele said. "The odds are slim, but it's not impossible."

"We also need to start digging into her life," Mel continued. "If someone wanted her dead, there has to be a reason."

Jared's mind drifted to the woman's story from the previous day. "What about the guy on the road? Could he somehow be a part of this? It never felt right to me that he would help her out of the vehicle and then abandon her."

"What guy?" Steele asked, his eyes lighting with curiosity. "Is there someone else I should be aware of? Perhaps someone I should be on the lookout for."

"Ms. Thompson claimed there was a man who rushed to her aid after she rolled her vehicle," Mel explained. "He pulled her out of the car and then instructed her to call for help. He didn't hang around to make sure she was okay or call 911."

"That's odd, right?"

"I would say so," Mel confirmed. "We thought it was odd yesterday, and that was before Ms. Thompson died. Now it seems downright suspicious."

"And you have no idea who this man is?"

"None. I think our first order of business is tracking him down, though. He seems like the obvious place to start."

"Agreed." Jared got to his feet. "We have to find him if we expect to get answers. He's the clear place to start."

"So ... let's do it."

FOUR

"I'm sorry but ... what?"

Harper thought she had a poker face when it came to her job, but nothing could've prepared her for the story Betty Miller was spinning from her driveway.

"It's true." Betty, a formidable woman in her seventies, folded her arms over her chest and defiantly met Harper's gaze. "The scarecrow is possessed."

"Oh, well ... ." Harper broke off as she scratched her nose and cast a furtive look toward Zander.

For his part, Zander managed to maintain control of his facial responses ... but just barely. "I'm going to need more specific information." He efficiently clicked the ballpoint pen he carried and flipped open the tiny notebook he kept in his pocket. "How did the haunting originate?"

Betty made an exaggerated face. "How do you think? Three days ago, I went out there, and the scarecrow started flapping his arms like he had ants in his pants or something. I thought for sure it was a trick of the eye ... Er, what are they called again?"

"Optical illusions," Harper volunteered helpfully.

"Right. Optical illusions." Betty bobbed her head. "I went to check it out, thinking the birds might've messed with the stuffing and the wind was making it move, but it spoke to me while I was out there and that was enough for me."

Zander furrowed his brow. "It spoke to you?"

"It asked about my day."

Confused, Harper rubbed her cheek. She had no idea what to make of the situation. "Are you certain someone else wasn't in the field with you?"

"I'm sure." Betty refused to back down and the expression she shot Harper promised mayhem if the woman continued to question her mental acuity. "The scarecrow is possessed."

"Okay, well ... ." Harper licked her lips. "We'll check out the scarecrow."

"You do that." Betty's tone told Harper she meant business. "My family is coming for Thanksgiving. I don't want that thing making a scene. That's my daughter's job. Get rid of it."

"We're on it."

LINDA PALTROW WAS unbelievably nervous when Jared and Mel sat the night nurse down to talk. She was essentially alone on the night shift for the bulk of the previous evening, and she was obviously worried she was about to be blamed for Vicky Thompson's death.

"Maybe I should call a lawyer." Linda licked her lips as she shifted on her chair. "I mean ... I didn't do anything, but I see on television that you should always have a lawyer when being questioned by the cops. Maybe I should call one.

"Of course, the only one I know is Lenny Dunham," she continued. "He's an ambulance chaser and he's dating my sister. I don't think he will be much help."

"You don't need to worry about a lawyer right now," Mel reassured her. He knew her from around town — Whisper Cove was a small place, after all — and he believed her reputation as something of a spaz was well earned. "We're not questioning you in conjunction with Ms. Thompson's death. We're questioning you because you were in charge of the floor last night, and we need to know if anyone who isn't on the visitor's list stopped in for a chat."

"Oh, well ... ." Linda chewed on her bottom lip as she tilted her head to the side. "I don't think so. You have to understand, it's quiet on the floor after ten and before five. That's the reason I volunteered for the shift even though I have seniority.

"I'm working on a book and I can write while everyone is asleep," she continued. "Once the meds are passed out at ten, I only need to do a few passes through the rooms. It's not as if this place is particularly happening right now, so the passes are quick."

"You checked on Ms. Thompson, right?" Jared queried. "You saw her after ten, didn't you?"

Linda nodded without hesitation. "I made a round at about midnight and she was sleeping soundly. I was in the middle of my rounds two hours later when the machines in her room started going off."

"Wait." Jared held up a hand to still her. "You weren't at your station when the machines alerted?"

"No. Why? Is that important?"

"I don't know." Jared was careful to keep his face neutral. "I need you to describe what happened, though."

"I don't know what happened." Linda's frustration bubbled up and she spoke more harshly than she intended. "I was down at the end of the hallway, in Jed Wharton's room, when I heard the first machine go off.

"Of course, that was the most isolated room on the floor, so I had to go around two bends to get back," she explained. "By the time I got to her room, she was coding. I called for a team and they tried for twenty minutes to save her ... but it didn't happen."

"Right." Jared was thoughtful as he rubbed the back of his neck. "Thank you for your time, Linda. We might have more questions later."

Linda exhaled heavily, relief evident. "Does that mean I can go?"

"Yeah, you can go."

Jared waited until Linda vacated the room to speak. "Do you find it a little convenient that Vicky Thompson coded when Linda happened to be away from the room?"

"I don't know if I would use the word 'convenient' or not," Mel hedged. "I find it suspect that it happened that way. It seems to me, someone had to be watching the floor and knew exactly when to slip into our victim's room and inject the cyanide into the bag."

"Yeah, that's exactly what I was thinking." Jared felt as if a ball of lead was sitting in the pit of his stomach. "This doesn't feel right."

"Oh, what was your first clue?"

"We're clearly missing the bigger picture here," Jared persisted. "Either someone was out to get Vicky Thompson because of something she did, some perceived slight, or ... ." He trailed off.

"Someone was out to get Vicky because he or she was afraid she knew something," Mel finished. "I'm right there with you. I don't like the odds."

"We need to look at those cameras," Jared said, straightening. "The footage might not help, but it can't possibly hurt."

"I happen to agree."

"HUH."

Harper tapped her chin as she circled Betty's demonic scarecrow, being careful to avoid a rut in the ground. It looked recently disturbed, as if someone had been digging, but it was a crop field so that didn't seem out of the ordinary.

"Do you see a ghost?" Zander asked.

"No."

"Do you see anything?"

Harper held her hands palms out and shrugged as she circled the staked figure. "It's kind of creepy, huh? Like a clown made out of straw."

"I hate it when you talk about clowns," Zander grumbled.

"You thought it was funny when you made fun of my clown fear."

"That's because I'm always up for making fun of you. It's nowhere near as much fun when you make fun of me."

"It's fun for me."

"We both know I'm the important one."

"Yeah, yeah." Harper made a dismissive waving motion with her hand as she eyed the scarecrow. "It's creepy, though, right?"

"Totally creepy," Zander agreed. "I don't understand why anyone would put something like this up on their property. It's as if they're purposely trying to scare themselves. I've never seen a horror movie with a scarecrow that ended well."

Harper bit back a laugh. "I think it's more apt to say that you've never seen a horror movie that ended well."

"True." Zander tilted his head to the side as he stared into the scarecrow's face. "Why would you put something like this in your field in the first place, though? I'm being serious. It's like asking for trouble."

"I think they're supposed to scare away birds."

"The birds have migrated for the season."

"Not all of them."

"Fine. The stupid birds are left."

Even though she knew she should be focusing on work, Harper couldn't stop herself from smiling at Zander's words. "I don't have a lot of knowledge on the intelligence of birds so I'm going to cede the argument to you."

"You should always cede every argument to me. Our lives would be much better if you did."

"I think you mean that your life would be much better if I did what you wanted," Harper countered. "My life would be much better if you would chill out a little bit."

"I have no idea what you're talking about." Zander tentatively touched the scarecrow's leg. "You're right. It's totally creepy. We should get out of here. We'll tell Betty she's cracked and the scarecrow isn't possessed, and then head back to town for hot chocolate. How does that sound?"

"The hot chocolate sounds good."

"We'll tell Betty she's cracked in a nice way, if that's what you're worried about."

"I'm not willing to tell her she's cracked at all right now," Harper countered. "While the scarecrow is creepy but seems normal, I can't shake the feeling that there's something different about it."

Zander was taken aback. "Like possessed different?"

"Like ... different." Harper's shoulders hopped as her frustration mounted. "I don't know how to explain it. I feel off ... and I think at least some of it has to do with this scarecrow."

Zander eyed his best friend for an extended beat. He wasn't sure if he should ask the question that had been plaguing him since the previous evening, but he wasn't one to bury questions and tiptoe around difficult situations. "Is some of your unease tied to what Jared said last night?"

The question caught Harper off guard. "What are you talking about?"

Zander had no intention of letting Harper weasel out of the conversation because she felt uncomfortable. "Quinn. You almost completely shut down when Jared brought up Quinn. I thought maybe you were off your game today because you were unnerved about what he said."

Harper balked. "Why would I be unnerved? Quinn died years ago. I'm not upset with Jared for bringing him up. I'm sure Mel mentioned what happened to Quinn when they were out there, and it was natural for Jared to bring it up."

"And you got all growly when he did bring it up," Zander argued. "You shut down, abandoned your dinner, and disappeared to take a bath so you wouldn't have to be around us. That wasn't a normal reaction. I mean ... it's a normal reaction for you whenever anyone brings up Quinn, but it's not a normal reaction for most people."

"What do you want me to say?"

Zander shrugged. "I don't know." That was the truth. He honestly didn't know what he expected from her when it came to Quinn Jackson. "I simply know that you spent years refusing to talk about Quinn, and I let you set the tone for that particular topic because I didn't want to hurt you."

It was rare for Zander to go an extended period of time without cracking a joke, but he was deathly serious now. "I never want to hurt you. Not ever. I knew that Quinn was a sore subject and I never pressed you, even though other people thought I should. I know you best, though, and I knew that was a mistake.

"Still, you and Jared have been together for months and you're great together," he continued. "I would never admit that to Jared because it's too much of an ego stroke, but you guys are amazing together. He loves you, listens to you, and goes out of his way to protect you. Don't ever tell him I said that."

Harper's lips twisted, although it was more of a grimace than a grin. "Your secret is safe with me."

"Jared makes you feel safe, which is what I want for you," Zander said. "Last night, though, you acted as if you didn't feel safe at all and shut down. I think it was weird."

Harper worked her mouth as she debated what to say. Finally, she went with her gut. "I don't want to talk about my ex-boyfriend with my current one. That seems somehow disrespectful."

"I think it's more than that."

"And I know it's not. I think I know my feelings better than you."

Zander wasn't convinced of that. He recognized Harper's brittle tone as a warning, though, so he opted to back off. "Fine. I simply want to make sure you're okay." He held up his hands in capitulation. "Do you want to do a full reading on the scarecrow just to be sure? I have some equipment in the truck."

"I think we should. Odds of it being evil are small, but I want to cover all our bases."

"I'll get the stuff."

"**AS YOU CAN SEE,** there aren't a lot of people who come in and out of the hospital after hours," Daniel noted as he stood behind Jared and Mel in the security room and watched the monitors. "That's Steven Lang. He's a nighttime janitor. That's Beverly Harper. She works on the sixth floor and was clearly late for her shift. I'll have to talk to her about that. I'm not sure who that gentleman is, but we can blow up the image and get a print for you."

Jared watched the security guard as he fast forwarded the footage, lifting a finger when a blur of movement flitted across the screen. "Back it up. Who is that?"

"I don't know," Daniel replied as he watched the man reverse the video. "It was too fast for me to see. That was after midnight, though. No one starts a shift at that time."

"Start from here," Jared instructed. "Watch him. He's coming from the visitor's parking lot, not the employee parking lot."

Mel was quiet as he watched the screen, allowing Jared to lead the way. He couldn't stop staring at the man in the video, though. There was something familiar about him ... although he couldn't put his finger on what.

"Does anyone recognize him?" Jared asked as the security guard paused the footage and tried to blow up the man's facial features. "He looks to be in his early thirties or so, sandy blond hair and a beard. It's too dark to get an eye color, but I'm going to estimate weight at about one hundred and ninety pounds or so."

"That sounds about right to me," Daniel acknowledged. "I don't know him. He doesn't work here. Although ... he looks familiar. I can't place him. It's on the tip of my brain, but elusive."

A memory snapped into place in Mel's head, causing his heart to roll and a gasp to escape. Jared was curious as he slid his eyes to his partner.

"Do you know who that is?"

Mel's mouth went dry as he nodded. "I'm afraid so."

"Who is it?"

"I ... ." Mel pressed the heel of his hand to his forehead, his heart rate picking up a notch. "It's impossible. I mean ... it's impossible. There's no way that's who I think it is."

Clearly intrigued, Daniel leaned forward. "Who do you think it is?"

"Um ... ."

"Oh, do you know who it looks like?" Daniel, clearly oblivious, remained focused on the screen rather than the police officers so he missed the distressed look on Mel's face. "It's the beard that threw me off. I could swear that's Quinn Jackson. Of course, he's dead, so it couldn't possibly be him."

Jared felt as if a fist was wrapping around his heart. "What?" He looked to Mel for reassurance, but the man's ashen features gave him pause. "That's Quinn Jackson?"

Mel swallowed hard and nodded. "It is. He doesn't look like a dead man either."

Jared swore viciously under his breath. "What could he possibly be doing here? He clearly hasn't been hiding in the woods for years recovering from his injuries. That means he left of his own volition. Why come back?"

The obvious answer washed over Jared before anyone else could speak and he pushed past Daniel so he could stride through the door.

"Harper."

"I HATE TO SAY IT, but this was a total waste of a morning," Zander complained as he walked through the cornfield with Harper after abandoning their scarecrow investigation. "There's no way that thing is possessed."

Harper couldn't help but agree with him, although her senses remained alert because she couldn't shake the feeling that something was about to go horribly wrong. "I don't know. Maybe there's something out there."

"I've seen *Children of the Corn*. If there's something out there, I don't want to know what it is."

"*Children of the Corn* isn't real."

Zander poked her side and twisted his face into something ugly. "Malachai."

"Knock that off."

Enjoying himself now, Zander committed to his role. "Malachai! Malachai!"

Harper squealed as she broke into a run to avoid him, her feet lightly skipping over an indentation so she didn't inadvertently pitch forward.

"He who walks behind the rows is going to eat you," Zander announced, a hint of a shadow catching his eye close to the truck they parked on the road. He pulled up short when he realized a man stood next to their vehicle, a smile on his face.

Zander wasn't psychic — or overly sensitive — but his blood ran cold when the man lifted his hand to his forehead to shield his eyes. It was a familiar mannerism, one he recognized from years before.

"Harper, wait." Zander meant to yell the words, but they came out as barely a whisper.

"If you think I'm buying you hot chocolate after you tried to scare me with your bad *Children of the Corn* impression, Zander, you're crazy." Harper barreled forward, clearly oblivious to the man — ghost would be more accurate — watching from the road. "I'm going to make you pay today, no matter how whiny you get."

"Harper." Zander's voice cracked. "Come back here."

Harper was too far gone. She finally lifted her head and saw the man, an unbidden smile rushing across her face. Zander sucked in a breath the moment she recognized the bearded individual, almost tripping over her own feet as the impossible smacked her across the face.

The man rushed forward and caught her before she hit the ground, however, and his smile was so bright it lit his entire face.

"Hello, Harper."

Harper openly gaped. "Quinn?"

"Long time no see."

FIVE

Harper's legs felt ungainly, as if they didn't belong to her body, and she pitched forward when her toe caught on a large rock as she approached the vehicle.

Zander, who increased his pace to make sure he was at her side when she came face to face with a man who supposedly died years before, caught her from behind before she could mar her pretty face on the gravel.

For his part, Quinn reacted out of instinct and thrust his hands out so he could grab Harper's arms and keep her from falling. The second Zander saw the man's hands on his best friend, he almost lost it.

"Don't touch her!" Zander slapped hard at Quinn's hands and jerked Harper's body backward, so she was pinned at his side.

Quinn, his eyes wide as he looked at Harper's face, managed a smile. It reflected marvel rather than annoyance at Zander's attitude, though. "I can't believe it's you."

Harper made a sound like a wounded animal in the back of her throat as she tried to find words.

"I think it's fair to say that we can't believe it's you either," Zander said finally, his eyes on fire. He felt exposed and alone, as if he somehow had to protect Harper from a man who could do her great bodily harm. In truth, he'd never been Quinn's biggest fan from the start. He never hated the man, of course, but he knew he wouldn't be hanging around so he didn't bond with him either. That was the exact opposite of how things went down with Jared. "Aren't you supposed to be dead?"

Quinn reluctantly drew his eyes away from Harper and focused on her shrill best friend. The smile he offered Zander was small but heartfelt. "Hey, Zander. You look exactly the same."

His arm firm around Harper's narrow waist so he could offer her support in case she fell, Zander decided the situation warranted a snippy attitude. "I can't say the same about you. The beard is a nice touch — kind of *Grizzly Adams* ... or *Duck Dynasty*, for that matter — and I can't ever remember you wearing flannel."

"Oh, well ... ." Quinn ran his hands over his shirt, as if searching for something.

"How are you here?" Harper's voice was full of awe when she finally managed to ask a question.

Quinn flicked his eyes back to her and smiled. "It's a long story."

"I think we have time to hear it," Zander barked. "If you try to tell us you've been wandering through the woods since your accident, though, just a warning ... we're not going to believe you."

"That's not what happened."

"Of course it's not what happened," Zander sneered. "Do you think I'm stupid enough to believe that's what happened?"

"I don't think anyone could ever mistake you for stupid."

The words were placating, but Zander hated the man's tone. His fury was palpable as he pinned Quinn with a hateful look. "I think you owe Harper an explanation. I mean ... did you fake your death? Where did you go? What are you doing here now? Harper is with someone, by the way. You can't just waltz back into her life. That's not going to happen."

"Zander." Harper's voice was stronger when she rested her hand on her friend's wrist. "You need to give him time to respond if you expect him to answer your questions."

"Oh, well, great." Zander sarcastically rolled his eyes. "I'm giving you time to answer the questions, Quinn. Knock yourself out."

Even though it was a surreal situation, even though it was like something out of a soap opera, Harper couldn't stop herself from laughing when Quinn fixed Zander with a pointed look. "Oh, it's as if I've been transported back in time."

"You haven't," Zander countered, firm. "Years have passed. Years where this guy let you believe he was dead. Don't forget that."

"I could hardly forget it, Zander." Harper's gentle tone was meant to be soothing. "Let him talk, though. I want to hear what he has to say."

"Thank you." Quinn smiled in gratitude as he dragged a restless hand through his hair. "I've been imagining how this conversation would go for what feels like forever."

"It *has* been forever," Zander snapped.

"Not really." Quinn rubbed his hand over his forehead, wiping at the beads of sweat pooling there. "So ... um ... I was in a car accident."

"That did it!" Zander threw his hands in the air and cursed a blue streak. "We already know about the car accident, dumbass." His fury knew no bounds. All he could think was that he had to protect Harper, keep this man away from her. It seemed an irrational fear and yet he felt it all the same. "If you think we're going to let you play with us, you have another think coming."

"I'm not trying to play with you, Zander." For the first time since reuniting with his former girlfriend, Quinn displayed a hint of anger. "Believe it or not, this isn't a game. I'm trying to explain things. It's not easy, though."

Zander refused to back down. "Do better than you're doing."

"Fine." Quinn exhaled heavily and held up his hands in defeat. "I was in a car accident. I remember it now, but I didn't for a long time. All I remembered was being confused, walking for what felt like forever. I woke up in a hospital, although it wasn't a Michigan hospital. It was a New York hospital."

Harper's forehead puckered. "I don't understand. How did you get to New York?"

"I honestly don't know." Helplessness clouding his features, Quinn held out his hands and shrugged. "My first firm memory after the accident is waking up in the hospital. To this day, I have no idea how I ended up there. The doctor said I was suffering from a head injury, and it seemed to be affecting my memory."

"Amnesia?" Zander's eyebrows flew up his forehead. "Are you claiming you had amnesia and that's why you put her through what you did? If so, I'm going to buy an entire library's worth of Lifetime movies on VHS and smack you upside the head with them."

Harper bit back a sigh as she tried to control her annoyance. Zander meant well. She knew that. The situation was rife with emotion, though, and it was likely to explode if she didn't keep a handle on things. "Zander, you're not helping. You need to calm your-self. He's doing the best he can."

"He's not doing anything!"

"He's trying. You won't let him get a sentence out."

"Oh, right. This is all my fault."

"It's no one's fault, Zander," Quinn countered. "No one is to blame for this. That's not how it went down. It's simply ... one of those things that happened. Some people might consider it a tragedy — or maybe even a travesty — but I've been coming to terms with it over the last few weeks."

"Let him tell the story," Harper ordered, her tone firm. "He clearly needs to tell it and I need to hear it."

"Fine." Zander desperately wished he had someone to help him muddle through this situation, even Jared who would likely melt down before taking over. He needed help. "I can't wait to hear the rest of this ridiculous story."

"It *is* a ridiculous story," Quinn confirmed. "Basically, it's an entire series of unbelievable events, one after the other."

"I still want to hear," Harper prodded. "Please."

"I was in the hospital for almost two months, although it wasn't because of physical injuries," Quinn volunteered. "I had a head injury, and a scar here." He pointed toward his chest. "The cut here was already healing — although the doctor said I was lucky to avoid infection because it was never stitched up properly — when I woke in New York.

"They ran a bunch of tests on me because I couldn't remember anything from before that hospital," he continued. "Not a single thing. I didn't remember my mother ... or my childhood ... or the years I was in college. My entire life was a blank slate."

"That must have been terrible," Harper lamented.

Quinn shrugged. "Honestly, it wasn't as terrifying as it probably should've been because I was recovering from a brain injury. I didn't react like a normal person would, or feel how a normal person would feel in a situation like that. I was simply numb."

"Maybe that was for the best."

"I don't know. It simply was." Quinn collected his thoughts. "After I recovered from my physical injuries, they moved me to the mental ward. I stayed there for six weeks so the psychiatrists and therapists could attempt to break through my brain fog."

"Did it work?"

"No." Quinn shook his head. "Basically, I recovered all my basic functions, but I still had no memory. I had no identity, no family, and no friends. I was in New York and I had no idea what to do with myself."

"And yet you still showed up here," Zander muttered under his breath.

Harper ignored the comment. "What happened?"

"My therapist took an interest in my case and wanted to write a paper for a medical journal," Quinn replied. "She helped me get a job — although it was a simple sales clerk position at a bookstore to start — and she helped me cope with what I was feeling and thinking.

"The thing is, I could make new memories, but nothing from my past was accessible and she was convinced there might be a chance of fixing that if we found the right therapy tool," he continued. "After about four weeks of working at the bookstore, it became obvious I was being underutilized and they promoted me to accountant, something I was pretty good at."

"You were always good with numbers," Harper confirmed. "I

remember when you helped Zander perfect our business plan for GHI."

"I didn't need help," Zander snapped.

"GHI." Quinn offered up a wide smile. "I didn't remember GHI until right now. How ... odd."

"You're still remembering things?" Harper had no idea how to respond to that. "That's ... I guess I don't understand."

"Yeah, I don't blame you." Quinn's smile was rueful. "I worked as the bookstore's accountant for two years before trading in the gig for a bigger one at an insurance company. I started making friends, developing a social circle, and generally getting on with my life.

"You have to understand, I didn't remember anything about this place ... or you," he continued. "I'm so sorry. I know what happened must have been awful for you."

Uncomfortable, Harper shifted from one foot to the other. "It wasn't easy."

"Try a living nightmare," Zander intoned.

"Through the years, I started getting weird flashes, although I didn't know what they meant at the time," Quinn explained. "The first was a flash of blond hair and a laugh. It was your laugh, although I didn't understand that at the time, for obvious reasons. The second flash was of my brother, when we were kids and before he died. We were screwing around in the backyard and having a good time."

"Did you understand what was happening?" Harper asked.

"I understood that they were probably memory flashes," Quinn confirmed. "I didn't understand why they were happening at that point in time, or how I was supposed to sort through them for clues about my old life. Even though I wasn't unhappy, I was desperate for answers."

"You obviously found them," Harper pointed out. "Was that recently?"

"Very recently." Quinn bobbed his head. "As it happens, I was sent to a conference at one of the bigger New York City hotels. While visiting, there just so happened to be a paranormal conference going on. I thought the people visiting were a bit wacky, but fairly entertaining.

"I was sitting in the bar having a drink with a few guests, laughing, when I told one of them I didn't believe in the paranormal," he continued. "Simply put, in my new world, I never had occasion to cross paths with anyone who believed in ghosts."

"I get that." Harper smiled. "Ghost hunting is an acquired taste."

Quinn returned the smile. "I guess. Anyway, when I mentioned I didn't believe in ghosts, one of the men pulled up an article from some scientific journal. It was about a team of ghost hunters who traveled to an asylum with a news crew ... and you and Zander were in the photograph accompanying the article."

Harper's mouth dropped open. "Oh. You saw that? Zander insisted we do a few interviews after the story broke big, but I wasn't sure it was a good idea." It was a lame thread to be snagged on, but Harper couldn't stop herself from veering. "I can't believe that's how you found us."

"It all came crashing back," Quinn supplied. "Er, well, your part came crashing back. Once I accessed memories of you, it was easy to draw upon other memories and I started remembering things at a fantastic rate. The first thing I remembered, though, was you."

"How long ago was that?" Zander asked.

"About three weeks."

"And you're just contacting her now?" Zander was huffy as he planted his hands on his hips. "Why did it take so long?"

"Because I had no idea how to do it," Quinn admitted. "I wanted to call her, I actually remembered her cell phone number, but my therapist thought that would be a rather jarring conversation. Harper already sees ghosts. If a dead guy called her, she might lose her mind."

"Yeah, that would've been weird," Harper agreed.

"I wanted to see her, but first I had to see my mother," Quinn explained. "It turns out she died two years ago. I didn't get to see her again."

"Oh, no!" Harper's made a disgusted face. "That's so unfair."

"Yeah, well, it is what it is." Quinn scratched his cheek, and Zander had the distinct impression that he did it simply because he was looking for something to do with his hand. The man was antsy. "I got to see some aunts and uncles, though, and cousins. That was good.

"When I finished there, I knew I wanted to see you," he continued. "I flew here yesterday, checked into the hotel downtown, and drove by the apartment you used to live in. Someone on the main floor told me you moved years ago, so I headed to your house. I was going to knock, but I panicked at the last second. I could hear voices inside — all male — and I didn't see you. I wasn't sure if you still lived there, perhaps maybe the woman who gave me information at the apartment complex was wrong, but that was the address supplied by the guy at the gas station."

"I still live there," Harper confirmed. "At least for a few weeks. I'm moving across the road, though."

"That's convenient." Quinn licked his lips. "I parked down the street this morning so I could watch the house. I know that sounds creepy, but I had no idea how I was going to approach you. The whole thing is ridiculous, like a movie or something, and I was afraid."

"I get that."

"I was going to give up and head back to the hotel when I saw you and Zander come out of the house," Quinn said. "You looked exactly the same, even more beautiful if that's possible. You were laughing at something Zander said to you.

"I know it's wrong, but I followed you," he continued. "I couldn't find the words to stop you before you drove away, so I followed. I saw you guys out in the field and decided to watch for a bit. When you started back, I figured it was now or never."

"It's okay." Harper nodded her head encouragingly. "I'm glad you waited."

"I had to see you."

"Yeah, well ... that story is simply unbelievable."

"Definitely unbelievable," Zander muttered under his breath, his head snapping to the left when he heard tires crunching against gravel. The relief he felt — like a soothing wave of warm water —

when he realized Jared was joining the show was profound. "Oh, look, it's Harper's other boyfriend."

"What?" Harper followed Zander's gaze, her eyes widening when she caught sight of Jared. He seemed to be in a hurry as he scrambled out of the cruiser. "Oh, I can't wait to tell him." She abandoned her conversation with Quinn without a second thought and bounced down the road so she could throw her arms around Jared.

The worry that had been consuming him since leaving the hospital disappeared as Jared tightened his grip on her. "Hey, Heart. I'm sorry to track you down but ... there's something I need to tell you. It's big."

"I think she already knows," Mel noted as he exited the police cruiser and pointed at Quinn. "That's the man right there."

"What?" Jared had been so fixated on Harper when they parked he'd barely noticed the figure standing next to Zander. "What is he doing here?"

"You knew he was here?" Confused, Harper shoved her hair away from her face. "How did you know he was here?"

"It's a long story." Jared stroked his hand over Harper's back and met Quinn's gaze head-on. "Has he said anything to you?"

Harper bobbed her head as she slowly drew away from Jared. "He told me the whole story. It's awful."

"Okay." Jared licked his lips. "What's the whole story?"

"He should probably tell you," Zander volunteered, his eyes speculative as they studied Quinn's profile. "It's quite the tale."

"That sounds like a good idea," Jared agreed, his hand extended in greeting as he stepped forward. "I'm Jared Monroe."

"Oh, where are my manners?" Harper's face flushed with embarrassment as she bounded between the two men. She was fluttery, and a bit off her game. "Quinn Jackson, this is Jared Monroe. He's my boyfriend."

"And they're moving in together," Zander added, smug. "They're in love and happy. Don't you even think of trying to ruin that."

SIX

Since Quinn's missing person file was still open, Mel and Jared instructed him to drive to the police station for questioning. Quinn readily did, promising Harper he would be in touch, and then sat for two hours to answer everything Jared and Mel threw at him. He even promised to provide phone numbers for hospital staff back in New York so they could check on his story.

He was so amiable, Jared found himself frustrated. He wanted to dislike the man on principle but, in truth, he realized jealousy was coming into play and it was something he wasn't exactly proud of. Still, he forced himself to remain calm when walking Quinn out of the building.

"So, that's it?" Quinn fixed Jared with a quizzical look.

"For now," Jared replied. "We'll call and verify the information you provided us with. Since it's coming up on a holiday weekend, it probably won't happen until after Thanksgiving. I'm going to guess, since you've legally been declared dead, you're going to have to jump through some hoops to have all that cleared. I'm not even sure what the process is."

"I'll contact an attorney and ask."

"That's probably a good idea."

Quinn stared hard into Jared's eyes. "You don't like me."

Jared was quick to respond. "I don't know you. I can't say if I like you if I don't know you."

"You're worried," Quinn countered. "You think I came back for Harper."

"Didn't you?"

"I came back to *see* her," Quinn clarified. "The idea that she was suffering because she thought I was dead was too much. It's been a long time, years. I've dated people since then. It's not the same as it was back then. Basically, I guess I'm trying to say that you don't have anything to worry about. I'm not here to ruin Harper's life. I thought she deserved the truth."

Jared wanted to believe him ... but he didn't. "Do I look worried?"

"You don't look happy."

"That's because I think it's a little convenient that you showed up in town on the same night a woman died."

"You already asked me about that," Quinn reminded him. "I told you. I had to check in with the hospital so they could run tests if I have further memory surges. My doctor in New York insisted on it. I left my information with the secretary. That's all on record."

"I don't understand why you did it in the middle of the night."

"Because I couldn't sleep. I was keyed up. I wanted to see Harper and yet I was afraid to spring my sudden resurrection on her. I would think you'd understand that."

"Yeah, well, we're going to check on the information you provided." Jared's tone was clipped. "Don't leave town until we get back to you."

"You don't have to worry about that. I'm nowhere near done with this town."

Jared didn't like the pointed comment. "What is that supposed to mean?"

"Nothing. It doesn't mean anything." Quinn held his hands out in a placating manner. "I don't want to get off on the wrong foot with you. It's obvious you're important to Harper. I don't want to intrude on that."

"Then don't." Jared kept his shoulders stiff as he held open the front door. "Don't be surprised if everyone in town knows you're back by tomorrow morning. Now that Zander knows, news is due to spread quickly."

"Yeah. He didn't look happy to see me either."

Finally, something we have in common, Jared internally muttered.

HARPER, ZANDER AND SHAWN sat around the living room table when Jared let himself into the house. Harper and Zander were in the middle of a story — Quinn's resurrection tale, of course — and Shawn was flabbergasted as he listened.

"Can you believe that?" Harper asked, her voice unnaturally high. "He had amnesia."

"Yes, it's like something out of a Lifetime movie," Zander drawled. "Not weird at all."

"Knock that off, Zander," Harper warned, extending a finger as she shifted her eyes to the door and offered Jared a smile in greeting. "How did things go?"

Jared had no idea how to answer. "I don't know. I've got nothing to compare the situation to." He heaved out a sigh as he sank onto the couch and rubbed his forehead. "Starting tomorrow, we have to track down the information he provided us with. Hopefully we'll know more then."

"You look tired." Harper leaned close and ran her thumb over Jared's cheek, her eyes cloudy. "Are you okay?"

The simple fact that she seemed so concerned relieved some of the weight Jared was carrying around on his shoulders. "I'm okay, Heart." He cupped the hand she held to his face. "I'm more worried about you."

"Why wouldn't I be okay?" Harper blinked several times in rapid succession. "You don't need to worry about me. I'm fine."

"I can see that." Jared chose his words carefully. He wasn't in the mood for a big battle. "I'm simply worried that this is a lot for you to deal with."

"I'm not going to pretend it's not weird." Harper rested her head on Jared's shoulder as he slipped his arm around her. He almost wanted to weep she felt so good pressed against his side. "When I first saw him standing there, it was like something out of a dream. He looked different, but kind of the same."

"Yeah." Jared stroked his hand down the back of Harper's head. "He seemed forthcoming when we interviewed him, provided us with hospital information and everything. He understands this won't be cleared up right away, that we need to make some calls, and with the Thanksgiving holiday coming up, that might be difficult."

"Yeah." Harper rested her hand on Jared's chest. "Is it wrong that I'm kind of angry?"

Jared's eyebrows winged up. "At me?"

"No. What did you do?"

"I ... nothing. At least last time I checked."

"I know it's wrong to be mad at Quinn because he couldn't control all of this, but I'm mad," Harper admitted. "It's not that I'm furious with him or anything — he's the victim in all this — but I'm irate at the situation. How could no one think to run Quinn's information in other states to see if they could match him to missing-person reports?

"I mean, think about it," she continued. "If New York had bothered to check reports out of Michigan, Quinn would have been returned here when he recovered. He probably would've gotten his memory back so much quicker and not suffered the way he did. Things would be totally different."

Jared swallowed hard. He didn't want to think of the way things would be different. "We can't go back in time and change that, Heart. It's probably best not to focus on it."

"I know." Still, she didn't look happy. "It's simply frustrating."

"I get that. It's a screwed-up situation and we're going to do our best to sort it out. You can't change the past, though. It's important to look toward the future."

"Wise words." Harper playfully poked his side. "Speaking of the future, I see pizza in ours because everyone was too excitable to cook. Is that okay with you?"

Jared nodded. "Pizza sounds great."

"YOU WERE HOLDING back at dinner."

Zander found Jared stuffing pizza boxes in a garbage bag shortly before ten. Shawn had already retired for the evening, Harper following suit. That left only Zander and Jared to clean up.

"I wasn't holding back at dinner," Jared argued. "I was merely ... thoughtful. It's a strange situation."

"It's an absolute nightmare," Zander corrected, causing Jared's lips to curve. "When I saw him standing next to the truck I couldn't believe it. I thought I was trapped in a nightmare. The look on Harper's face ... ."

Jared pressed the heel of his hand to his forehead. "Did she look happy?"

Zander slid him a sidelong look. "No. She seemed confused."

"Confused and then happy?"

"No. What is your deal? You've been acting weird all night."

"Oh, really? I can't believe that." Jared's tongue was practically dripping with sarcasm. "Why would the fact that my girlfriend's former boyfriend just came back from the dead make me weird?"

"Don't scowl like that," Zander automatically instructed. "You'll give yourself wrinkles."

"I don't really care about wrinkles."

"Everyone cares about wrinkles."

"I don't." Jared viciously shoved the boxes into the garbage bag. "I care that the man Harper was with until she thought he died is back and I'm terrified that means she's going to end our relationship."

Zander's mouth dropped open. "Oh, dude."

"Just ... don't." Jared pinched the bridge of his nose. He felt like an idiot ... and then some. He hated looking vulnerable, especially in front of Zander. Even though he admonished Harper to the contrary, he wanted to go back in time twenty-four hours and forget any of this had ever happened. "I know I'm being an ass. You don't have to point it out to me."

"You're not being an ass." Zander slowly lowered himself to the ground, his back to the refrigerator, and fixed Jared with a pointed look. "You can be an ass when you want to be — usually when you're telling me what to do — but, in general, you're not an ass."

"How great."

"Yes, it's truly lovely," Zander drawled, his lips curving into a smug smile. "Harper loves you. Don't doubt that."

"Except the guy she cared about before me is back," Jared grumbled, dropping to the floor so he could sit across from Zander. "I know you said she didn't care about him like she does me but ... I'm afraid." It was hard for him to admit it. "I've felt sick all day. I'm so afraid I'm going to lose her now that I can't even concentrate."

"You're not going to lose her." Zander wasn't often sympathetic to the plight of others, but Jared's emotional distress touched him. "She loves you. She never loved Quinn. I've told you that a hundred times."

"Yes. It was easier to accept when I thought he was dead. Now he's back and Harper is ... thrilled ... that he's not dead. Do you know how that makes me feel?"

"Annoyed that he isn't dead?" Zander queried.

"Yes, and that makes me a horrible person. I was happier when I thought that man was dead. That makes me the worst sort of jerk."

"It does not." Zander offered a dismissive wave. "I don't want him back either. I never liked him."

"You're fine being a jerk, though," Jared pointed out. "I'm a good boyfriend ... and I should want what's best for Harper. You saw the look on her face. She's ecstatic that he's back."

"No, she's happy that he's not dead," Zander corrected. "That's a different thing entirely. She's numb, in shock. All she knows is that the guilt she felt over keeping Quinn in Whisper Cove when he wasn't all that happy here can be put away.

"Now, don't get me wrong, a different sort of guilt is going to slip in when she has a good night's sleep," he continued. "She's going to blame herself for Quinn going through years of turmoil not knowing who he was. She'll blame herself for not realizing he was suffering from amnesia and was out there needing guidance even though it's ridiculous to think anything of the sort. She'll get over it eventually, though.

"You're looking at this the wrong way," he said. "She doesn't want to get back together with Quinn. You can't think things like that. I swear, other than him grabbing her arms to keep her steady when she almost tripped, they didn't touch one another. There were no hugs or kisses. It was almost ... clinical."

Zander's description of the meeting gave Jared hope. "That's something, right?"

"She loves you, Jared. You have to know that."

"I *do* know that." Jared bobbed his head in confirmation. "I can't help but wonder if Quinn's return shifts things for us, though. They were together first."

"They wouldn't have survived. How many times do I need to tell you that?"

"I want to believe you. The thing is, you said it yourself, Quinn's death turned him into something of a martyr in Harper's mind. She elevated him onto a pedestal that didn't exist before his disappearance."

"She did, and I was frustrated when it happened," Zander acknowledged. "The thing is, even when that happened, it wasn't love she was feeling. It was guilt. Harper has never loved anyone but you. I mean ... she loves me, but not in a romantic way. You're the only one to get that lucky."

Jared didn't want to admit it — insecurity wasn't a normal emotion for him — but Zander's words gave him hope. "I'm probably just projecting. I've never been in this situation before."

"Nobody but soap opera heroines have been in this situation," Zander said. "All you have to do is remain mellow and calm. Harper is going to be on a roller-coaster of emotions for a good forty-eight hours, and then she's going to come screaming back to reality."

"And what reality is that?"

"That Quinn can't be trusted." Zander was matter-of-fact. "I didn't trust him before he disappeared. He was always smarmy and seemed to be up to something ... although I could never figure out what. I don't expect that to change now that he's returned."

"If his amnesia story holds up, he could very well be a different person," Jared pointed out. "I've heard of traumatic brain injuries that changed a person's personality. We might be looking at that here."

"Perhaps," Zander mused. "I don't think so, though. He had the exact same personality I remembered on display this morning. Sure, it was all wrapped up in a bunch of 'golly gee, I can't believe this happened' and 'one of the first things I remembered was you' statements, but I still don't trust him."

Jared gave Zander a considering look before letting out a shaky sigh. "I don't trust him either. I just assumed it was because of jealousy, which was hard to admit even to myself. He makes me uneasy, as if everything Harper and I have been building is contingent upon what he says and does."

"That's not true." Zander was firm. "Trust me. Harper is still dealing with shock because she can't believe he's alive. She'll return to reality quickly, though, and that future you guys have been planning will be just as important as ever."

"I hope so."

"I *know* so." Zander awkwardly patted Jared's knee to offer comfort. "Trust me. This is all going to be okay. You're still going to move in April."

Jared made a face. "December. We're moving next month."

"You just made more lines on your face. That's not good."

"Yeah, yeah." Jared rolled to his feet before extending a hand to help Zander up. "You'll watch Harper for me when I'm at a work, right? If Quinn is up to something, I don't want anything happening to her."

"Oh, you don't have to worry. As long as Quinn Jackson is back in town, I'll be watching her like a Kardashian watches a television camera. You don't have to worry about that."

"Thank you."

"No, thank you." Zander's smile was serene. "I finally have someone to share my Quinn hate with. The day is looking up."

. . .

HARPER WAS IN BED, a furniture catalog open on her lap when Jared walked into the bedroom. He wordlessly stripped out of his shirt and pants before crawling into bed next to her.

"What are you looking at?"

"Kitchen tables," Harper replied, lifting his arm so she could snuggle in at his side. It was such an endearing action that Jared couldn't stop himself from clutching her a little tighter than normal.

"Do you see something you like? We can get whatever you want."

Harper's eyes were curious as they shifted to Jared's face. "I'm still looking. I thought we would decide together. That's one of the joys of moving in together, right?"

"Yeah." Jared's fingers were soft as they caressed Harper's cheek. "I love you."

Harper's eyebrows shifted higher. "I love you, too. What's wrong?"

"Nothing. I just ... it's been a long day."

"It has," Harper agreed. "Do you want me to put the catalog away and shut off the light? You obviously need sleep."

"No, I want to look at tables with you." Jared meant it. "Turn back to the beginning of the section and show me some options."

"Okay." Harper was happy to acquiesce. "For the space we're dealing with, I think a rectangular table would be better than a round one. Maybe with a buffet at the end for that one wall."

"I know what you're talking about." Jared kissed Harper's forehead and briefly pressed his eyes shut. He honestly didn't care about the table. The fact that she was excited to look with him was more than enough to get him through the night. This closeness was all he needed. "Do you know what kind of material you want the table to be made out of?"

"Reclaimed wood."

"That's specific."

"I've always liked reclaimed wood," Harper explained. "I want a nice table with prairie benches on two sides and chairs on either end. Although, now it occurs to me that you might not like that."

"I have no problem with that." Jared stared at the table on the catalog page. "That's really cool. I think we would have a good time with that table."

"See, I think you're anticipating cooking up something more than food on that table," Harper teased. "I'm a good girl. I don't do things like that. The kitchen table is for eating."

"Did I say otherwise?"

"No, but I know how your mind works."

"And I know how your mind works." Jared poked her side as she squealed and squirmed, rolling her to her back so he could mock wrestle her to the mattress. "How is your mind working tonight?"

"I don't know," Harper teased. "You're going to have to experiment to find out."

"I'm always up for experimenting."

"You are good that way."

"Let's see what I can come up with, shall we?"

"That's what I was hoping for."

Harper squealed again when Jared tickled her, ignoring the catalog that fluttered off the bed and fell to the floor. She laughed so hard that she was gasping for breath when Jared tickled her, although the sound changed to a satisfied groan when he added a kiss to the mix.

"I love you so much," he whispered as the game turned fervent. "I mean it. I've never loved anyone like I love you."

"I love you, too. Always. Now ... keep experimenting. I'm nowhere near done with you tonight."

"Yes, ma'am."

SEVEN

"How were things last night?" Mel looked up from his computer the next morning when he heard Jared entering the office they shared. He'd been worried about his partner the entire night, and worry made him antsy.

"Good morning to you, too," Jared said dryly.

"Good morning. How did things go last night? How was Harper?"

Jared let loose a sigh as he poured himself a mug of coffee from the communal pot before shuffling to his desk and sinking into the rolling chair. "It was okay. I mean ... it was a normal night with a few conversations about Quinn. Shawn obviously wanted to hear the story, so Harper and Zander told it from the beginning for his benefit. Then we ordered pizza and went to bed."

Mel's face was blank. "That's it?"

"That's it."

"That is so not what I was expecting."

"Yeah, it's not what I was expecting either," Jared admitted, wrinkling his nose when he sipped the coffee. "Ugh. Sometimes less is more, man. This is so strong it's liable to knock me over."

"Suck it up." Mel was blasé. "It will put hair on your chest.

59

According to Zander, men don't want hair on their chests these days for some reason, but real men have hair on their chests."

"That's good to know." Jared smiled as he flicked his attention to his inbox. "Did we get anything good overnight?"

"As a matter of fact, we did." Mel turned serious. "Henrietta Fisher stopped by this morning. She was out by County Line Road two days ago. She didn't think much of it when she heard the driver only had minor injuries, but she saw a man help Vicky Thompson from her vehicle.

"After she heard about Ms. Thompson's death, she thought she should come in and describe what she saw," he continued. "It wasn't much of a description, but I thought you might find it interesting."

Despite himself, Jared was intrigued. "Lay it on me."

Mel picked up a sheet of paper and read aloud. "Five-foot-eleven. Blond hair shot through with brown streaks. Jeans. Flannel shirt. Beard. Black sedan that looks like a rental car."

Jared's heart skipped a beat. "Are you serious?"

"I am."

"But ... no way."

"Yes, way." Mel was firm as he nodded. "Henrietta described Quinn Jackson to a tee. I don't think we can ignore that fact."

"That means we have to question him again." Jared wasn't sure how he felt about the turn of events. He didn't trust Quinn. Being around the man was a true test of his patience. "I guess we have no choice."

"We definitely don't," Mel agreed. "The coroner confirmed cyanide in Vicky's system. She was murdered. Quinn just happened to be at the hospital that night, which is a bit too convenient for me. We have no choice but to question him."

"Then I guess we should get on it."

"That's the plan."

"OH, MY GAWD!"

Molly Parker, her hair dyed a bright shade of orange that was a holdover from Halloween, practically attacked Harper when the woman walked through the front door of GHI shortly after breakfast.

"You have to tell me absolutely everything," Molly enthused as she helped Harper remove her coat. "I mean ... he was supposed to be dead. How come he's not dead? How was your reunion? Was it like something straight out of a movie?"

"Yes, it was," Zander answered before Harper could find her voice. He trailed behind her, his countenance pouty, and it was clear to anyone who knew him that he was being anything other than sweet and supportive. "It was straight out of a horror movie."

Molly scalded Zander with a quelling look. Technically, Zander was her boss. She wasn't much for being bossed around, though, so she essentially did whatever she wanted. That wasn't about to change today, especially given the gossip she was convinced would be flying fast and furious within seconds. "You're such a joy."

"I *am* a joy," Zander countered, pushing past her and fixing his full attention on the fourth member of their ghost-hunting group, Eric Tyler. "Did you look over the information I sent you last night?"

"What information did you send him?" Harper asked, curious. "You didn't tell me you were sending Eric information."

"That's because our afternoon was derailed yesterday," Zander shot back. "Once Quinn returned to our lives, you forgot about work. As for what I sent Eric, it was simply video footage and EMF readings that we took near the scarecrow yesterday. It's not a big deal."

"Oh." Harper furrowed her brow. "Did you find anything?"

"Actually, I found a few interesting readings in the data Zander supplied," Eric replied. "For starters, the ectoplasm reading was through the roof. That was on top of the ... ."

He didn't get a chance to finish what he was about to say because Molly planted her hands on her hips and glared at him. "We're not done talking about Quinn yet. We can get to the boring ectoplasm stuff later."

After a tumultuous start, Eric and Molly started dating on the sly a few months before. The relationship hadn't exactly been smooth sailing, but the duo showed no signs of splitting. They had strong chemistry ... and that included fighting.

"Well, excuse me for living," Eric drawled.

"You're excused," Molly said sweetly. "Now it's time to focus on Harper, though. I want to know what she has to say. We'll talk about your ectoplasm later."

"Fine, darling," Eric snapped. "We'll do what you want to do. Like always."

"That's exactly what I want to hear." Molly beamed as she turned her full attention back to Harper. "I want to hear everything. How was the reunion? Did you cry? Did he cry? Where has he been? I heard he had amnesia? That is just so ... Hollywood."

"That's not necessarily a good thing," Zander grumbled, earning an appreciative look from Eric. It was clear they were on the same side.

"I don't know how much there is to tell you," Harper hedged. "It sounds to me as if you've heard the entire story already. How did you hear it, by the way?"

"Everyone in town is talking about it," Molly answered, her patience clearly wearing thin. "That's all anybody can talk about. It's not every day that someone comes back from the dead, though, so that's to be expected."

"I guess." Harper dropped her purse on her desk and shrugged. "Where do you want me to start?"

"From the beginning."

"Okay, but I don't think it's going to be as grand a story as you believe."

"I'll be the judge of that."

QUINN DIDN'T SEEM surprised to find Mel and Jared waiting for him in the hotel lobby when he made his way downstairs for breakfast. In fact, he'd been expecting them, so it was more a confirmation than anything else.

"Have you guys eaten?" He pointed toward the dining room. "They have a great breakfast buffet."

"That sounds like a good idea," Mel said. "We'll get breakfast and then we have a few more questions."

"I figured you would."

Quinn picked a table in the corner so the three men could have privacy, and Jared was the first to join him after filling his plate. In truth, Jared wasn't overly hungry. He wanted to appear relaxed, though, and the best way he knew to do that was to eat.

"The food is good," Jared noted as he cut a sausage link. "I didn't realize the food here was this great. I'll have to keep that in mind over the winter."

"Yeah, Harper isn't much of a cook," Quinn noted. "She has other attributes, though, so the lack of cooking skills isn't terrible."

Quinn's offhand comment set Jared's teeth on edge. "Zander usually cooks. However, we were running late this morning and I had to skip breakfast."

"You guys live with Zander?"

"It's ... complicated." Jared mashed his eggs and hash browns together, mostly so he had something to do with his hands besides wrapping them around Quinn's neck. "Our living situation is transitional until the second week of December."

"Meaning?"

"Meaning that Harper and Zander still technically live together, although Shawn and I spend every night over there. Once Harper and I move — we're still waiting for painters and new carpet — then Shawn and Zander will own the old house and Harper and I will own the new."

"I see." Quinn's reaction was hard to read. He was good at shuttering his emotions. "How long have you been seeing each other?"

"Since the spring."

"That's not very long."

"It was long enough to convince both of us we want to be together forever," Jared argued. "We're happy. Harper is thrilled to have a place of her own to decorate."

"See, when I was here before, Harper *did* have her own place,"

Quinn pointed out. "It was a small apartment, but it was her own space. Zander and Harper didn't live together back then."

Jared searched his memory. Now that Quinn mentioned it, he remembered Zander explaining that he was worried about his best friend after Quinn's purported death. She spent all her time in the woods looking for a ghost that didn't exist, to the point where she lost weight and Zander demanded the new living arrangements so he could keep an eye on her.

"I believe they bought the house together several months after your accident," Jared explained. "They knew they wouldn't stay together forever, but they actually enjoy being on top of one another."

"Was it difficult for you to convince Harper to move away from Zander?"

"No. I actually talked to Zander first to make sure he was okay with it. When the house became available, it seemed too good to pass up. It's got a nice river view and is directly across the road from Zander. That means Harper and Zander can still spend an exorbitant amount of time together, but Shawn and I can still have our private space. It's the perfect situation."

"I'm glad things are working out well for Harper," Quinn said, holding up his hands when Jared pinned him with a suspicious look. "No, really, I am. I know you don't believe that because ... well, if I were in your position, I wouldn't believe me either. I'm not here to hurt her, though."

"Why are you here?"

"Because I had to see her. I can't blindly move forward now that I actually remember my past. I thought I owed it to her to explain what happened now that I understood things myself. That only seemed fair."

Jared wanted to argue the point, but he knew Quinn wasn't wrong. Nothing the man had said wasn't truthful. It would've been mean to punish Harper and keep her from the truth. Only a truly terrible person would do anything of the sort.

"I'm sorry." Jared held up his hands in capitulation. "I don't mean to jump all over you. This situation is ... hard. I've never been through anything like this before, so I can't stop my hackles from jumping all over the place."

"And I don't blame you." Quinn's eyes reflected sincerity. "I was put off by your attitude yesterday, until I spent the evening in my hotel room thinking about things from your point of view. I wouldn't be happy if I were you either. In fact, I wouldn't be able to stop myself from questioning the former boyfriend's motivations.

"With that in mind, here are mine," he continued. "I don't want to hurt Harper. I don't want to steal her from you. I understand she's built a life and I'm not part of it. If you want to know if I still have feelings for her, the answer is yes. But ... I don't know if those feelings are real or if they simply popped up because I suddenly remembered my past. They could completely disappear once I've settled into my new reality."

"I guess I never considered that," Jared mused, rubbing his chin. "Once the memories came back, you were probably flooded with emotions at the same time. That had to be difficult."

"It was. It was terrifying, and not just because of Harper. You should know, the first thing I did was track down my mother. It sounds trite, but I wanted my mommy. She was already gone, though."

Jared cleared his throat to buy himself a moment. "That must have been terrible for you."

"It was worse for her. She died thinking she was going to see me on the other side, that I was already dead, and I'm still here. It's a bitter pill to swallow."

"I bet."

"After I dealt with my family, then my mind turned to Harper," Quinn explained. "It wasn't that I didn't think of her before. I don't want to make it sound as if she was the last person on my mind. That's not fair or true.

"It was weird, though," he continued. "I picked up the phone to call, but that didn't seem right. Can you imagine how she would've reacted if a dead guy called her? I knew I had to see her in person. However anxious I was, though, my family came first."

"I don't blame you for that," Jared said. "In your particular position, I would've gone to my family first, too."

"What about if it were you?" Quinn queried. "Would you have gone to your family or Harper first?"

Jared shrugged, noncommittal. "I don't know."

"I think you do know."

"Fine. I do know." Jared's blue eyes were clear when they locked with Quinn's darker orbs. "I would've gone straight for Harper. No force on this planet could've kept me from her. She is my family."

Quinn nodded, his expression thoughtful. "Yeah. I thought you might say something like that. You need to know, I'm not here to take Harper from you. I don't believe she belongs with me. I still needed to see her. I think we both needed it so we could start moving past what happened."

"And how are you going to move past things? Are you going back to New York?"

"Probably, although that's not set in stone," Quinn replied. "My family is in Seattle. They want me to go there. There's a woman in New York, we were dating when I remembered. It's not exactly an easy situation."

"Where is she now?"

"She's still there. We'd only been dating two months when all this went down. She's upset that I'm visiting an old girlfriend, but I can't pretend Harper doesn't exist to make her happy. Besides, I need to see Harper for me, so I can get past all this."

"I think you're handling it to the best of your ability," Jared admitted. "It's a tough situation and there is no correct answer. However, I do have another question."

"Okay."

"Two days ago, did you go out to the area where you wrecked your car?"

Quinn turned sheepish. "I did. I had to see it. I thought maybe it would jar my memory some. I don't remember anything from the weeks after the accident. Still, that part is a blur. I don't know how I got into the woods or how I left the county. None of it makes sense. How did you know I was out there?"

"Because another woman had an accident, and witnesses described the man who helped her out of her vehicle as having blond hair with brown undertones, jeans, flannel, a beard, and a black rental car."

A muscle ticked in Quinn's jaw. "Are you asking if that was me?"

"Yes."

"Well, it was." Quinn's cheeks flooded with color. "I was out there looking around the area. It seemed familiar, but not the same. I don't know how to explain it. I was looking for a trigger, and then as if I was caught in a bad movie, I saw the car coming down the road.

"I didn't think much of it at first," he continued. "Then I saw the deer. It reminded me that I saw a deer on the road before my accident. The car rolled and landed in the ditch. Before I realized what was happening, I was running. I helped the woman out of the car and that was it."

"You didn't do anything wrong helping her," Jared noted. "You did the right thing helping her. Why didn't you stay and call the police, though? Why didn't you wait to make sure that she got help?"

"Honestly? I panicked." Quinn shook his head, as if shame was washing over him in waves. "I realized that if the cops saw me, it would become a big story. 'Local man back from the dead' and all that. I didn't want Harper to find out I was back that way, so I took off. It was the coward's route and I regretted it as soon as I got back to the hotel, but I couldn't stop myself."

"I can actually see that reaction and sympathize with it," Jared said. "My problem is, the woman from that accident died in the same hospital you visited later that night. She was poisoned."

Quinn's mouth dropped open. "What? Wait ... are you suggesting I did that?"

"I'm suggesting you were one of the only people to enter that hospital after dark that night," Jared responded. "It seems suspicious when you couple it with your hospital visit and a car accident rescue you don't want to take credit for."

"What would my motive be?"

"I don't know." Jared opted for honesty. "I can't figure out what your motive would be. I can't rule you out, though, either. I don't believe in coincidences."

"Well, you need to start." Quinn's eyes flashed with something dangerous. "I didn't hurt that woman. I didn't even get her name. I was shaken after seeing the accident, wondering if my car did the same thing. My mind was jumbled, and I did the wrong thing. That doesn't mean I came back to murder her later that night."

Jared studied Quinn's face for a long beat. He seemed sincere, but Jared wasn't the type to believe anything without proof. "Well, for your sake, I hope you're telling the truth. If you had something to do with that woman's death, I won't hesitate to arrest you."

"I had nothing to do with her death. I swear it."

"Then you have nothing to worry about."

EIGHT

Jared and Mel headed to the garage after finishing breakfast. They asked Quinn a series of questions — all of which he answered without stumbling or whining — and then departed the hotel, leaving him with an admonishment that he wasn't to leave town until they told him otherwise.

Mel waited until they were in the cruiser to ask the obvious question. "Do you think he's telling the truth?"

Jared hated being put on the spot. "I don't know. I'm not sure my judgment is unbiased in this particular case."

"Because of Harper?"

"Of course. Now that Quinn is back, I feel irrationally territorial. I want to lock him in a room and never let him see her."

"I don't think that sounds irrational," Mel hedged. "It doesn't necessarily sound healthy, don't get me wrong, but I don't think it sounds irrational."

"Of course it's irrational." Jared's agitation was on full display as he tapped his fingers on the car dashboard. "She's never done anything to make me believe she's not completely loyal and trustworthy. Plus, this situation is beyond her control. She didn't ask him to come back here."

"You and Quinn talked for a long time while I was going through the buffet line. Did he say anything of note?"

"No. It was more of the same. I mean ... I get it. If the story is true, I don't think I would've reacted any differently. Well, except for the fact that I would've gone straight for Harper because it would've killed me to be away from her. I don't think it's possible for me to forget Harper, though."

Mel smirked. "You are a bit codependent."

"I don't care. I'm fine being codependent."

"I've noticed." Mel wanted to help his partner, ease the man's worry. He had no idea how to go about it, though. "We need to track down Quinn's information, and we need to do it in a way that can be independently verified so we can be sure he didn't hire people to say what he wanted them to say."

"Fair enough."

"Before then, though, we need to look over Vicky Thompson's car. Ned Patterson called from the garage and said they found something in the trunk that we should see."

"And who is Ned Patterson?"

"He owns the tow service that the township contracts to handle wrecks. In single-vehicle accidents like this one, it's common for him to go over the car and then leave it to the insurance company to make a decision. Once Vicky died, I asked him to give the car a good once-over just to be on the safe side."

"That was smart."

"Well, I guess it depends on what he found. He says we need to see it to believe it."

"At least that gives us a place to start," Jared noted. "As it stands, we need a direction to look. Vicky Thompson's death caught us completely off guard, and when you add Quinn to the mix, it's a real cluster of crap."

"That's for sure." Mel shifted his thoughtful eyes to Jared. "Did you warn Quinn away from seeing Harper?"

"No."

"You didn't? How come?"

"Because Harper is an adult and I wouldn't do that to her," Jared replied honestly. "She has a right to see Quinn, hear what he has to say. I'm not her keeper."

"You kind of want to be her keeper, though, don't you?"

"Not really. I like that she's her own person."

"But?"

"But ... I don't trust this guy," Jared admitted, the invisible fist wrapped around his heart easing its grip when he finally said the words out loud to someone other than Zander. "I can't shake the feeling that something else is going on here."

"Like he didn't really get hit in the head and suffer from amnesia?"

"I don't know. I mean ... that's possible. I've read stories where that really happened and thought they were crazy, but I still believed them."

"So, what's the problem?"

"The problem is that the woman I love is caught up in this story and I don't like it," Jared replied. "I want to keep her safe more than anything. I can't help wondering if Quinn is a danger to her. Then, when I think hard about that, I get angry at myself because I have no reason to think Quinn is a danger to her. It's more that he's a danger to my emotional well-being. It doesn't seem fair."

"When your heart gets involved, son, sometimes what's 'fair' goes out the window."

"I know. I have to be careful, though. If I put my foot down and demand Harper say away from him, she'll get angry and see him out of spite. That's the opposite of what I want. If she starts shutting down or closing me off, then Quinn will have succeeded in driving a wedge between us."

"You don't know that he's trying to put a wedge between you."

"I don't. He says all the right things."

"You're still suspicious, though."

"I am, and I'm not the only one. Zander is suspicious, too."

"Zander never liked Quinn," Mel pointed out. "He thought Quinn was trying to steal Harper away from him. He was freaking irrational during the height of Harper and Quinn's relationship."

"You can say what you want about Zander — and he is a real pain in the keister — but he would never purposely hurt Harper." That was one of the few things Jared never questioned. "He loves her too much. He's suspicious of Quinn because he wants to protect her."

"I agree that Zander would never purposely hurt her. That doesn't necessarily mean he's right. He's fought you a time or two for Harper's affections. Don't forget that."

"I won't. He's my ally this time, though. I can feel it."

"Just don't let him talk you into doing something crazy."

"I'll do my best."

"**THAT IS THE** craziest story I've ever heard." Molly was agog when Harper wrapped up her tale. "Can you believe that story, Eric?"

For his part, the taciturn computer and equipment expert was less enthralled with the romantic amnesia saga than his lady love. "I don't believe one bit of that story," he replied, ignoring the way Molly's eyes fired. "That's the most ridiculous thing I've ever heard."

"Thank you!" Zander threw his hands up in the air. "Finally! Someone sees what I see."

Harper bit the inside of her cheek to keep from exploding at Zander's bad attitude. "And what do you see?"

"That story is ridiculous," Zander replied without hesitation. "There's no way — especially given the technology we have today — that a New York hospital wouldn't send out one of those APB things to get an identity on some random injured dude who showed up without identification or memory of who he was."

"An APB is a tool that cops utilize, but I don't disagree with you," Eric said. "It's not the sixties ... or even the eighties. The people at the hospital would've taken a photo of Quinn and passed it around through some hospital network that I'm sure exists. Since Quinn's photograph would've been all over the news here, all it would've taken is one person at any southeastern Michigan hospital seeing him and the truth would've come out."

"I don't disagree with that," Harper admitted. "The thing is, he said it was weeks. He can't remember what happened in the time between getting in the accident here and ending up there, but it was weeks.

"Quinn was front-page news for a week here," she continued. "I was furious when the newspapers stopped reporting on him. Once that died down, though, it was essentially as if he never existed. If it took him weeks to get to New York, then maybe the people seeing the bulletin at Michigan hospitals simply forgot about Quinn because so much time had passed."

"I don't see how any of this is possible," Eric persisted. "How did no one notice that guy walking around with a head injury? He also had a chest wound and was bleeding. He didn't walk to New York. There's no way. That means someone drove him. Who?"

"I don't know." Harper held her hands out as frustration washed over her. "I've spent a lot of time thinking about it since he told me his story. He can't remember anything from the time he was in the accident to the time he woke up. When he did wake up, he remembered nothing from his past. Maybe there's something there, but he hasn't realized it yet because the information is something of a deluge."

"I guess." Eric rubbed the back of his neck and did his best to ignore the eye daggers Molly shot in his direction. "I still don't think the story makes sense."

"Well, I do." Molly folded her arms over her chest and practically dared Eric to argue with her. "I'm an expert on amnesia."

"How?" Eric challenged. "Who do you know who has amnesia?"

"Um ... Laura ... and Tad ... and Jack ... and Nick ... and Felicia."

Eric's face remained blank. "Who are these people?"

"Soap opera characters," Zander replied without hesitation. "Amnesia is big on soaps."

"That only further proves that this guy is making up his story," Eric persisted. "I mean ... amnesia? It's so ridiculous."

"I think it's romantic," Molly shot back. "He lost his memory for five years, started a new life, and when he came back, he immediately sought out Harper. How is that not a romantic story?"

"He didn't immediately seek me out," Harper hedged. "He went to find his mother first. She died a few years ago, though."

"Oh." Molly pressed her hand to the spot above her heart. "That's even more romantic."

"That's not romantic." Zander was at the end of his rope. "Besides, in case you've forgotten, Harper already has a boyfriend. She's moving in with him. There's no room for Quinn in her life."

"Oh." Realization dawned on Molly's perky features. "I didn't even consider that. How is Jared taking things?"

"He's fine," Harper replied. "He had to question Quinn so they could close his file, but he's fine otherwise. Why wouldn't he be okay?"

Zander rolled his eyes at his best friend's naïveté and almost choked on his tongue when he saw Quinn approaching GHI's glass front door. "Oh, you've got to be kidding me."

"What?" Harper asked, her eyebrows drawing together when she saw Quinn opening the door. "Oh, I ... oh."

"Yes, oh," Zander muttered, his temper ratcheting up a notch.

"Who is that?" Molly asked, confused. "Wait ... is that him?" She was almost giddy as she jumped to her feet. "I can't believe he's really here."

"And I don't think now is the time to make a scene," Eric noted, grabbing Molly by the back of her neck and drawing her against him. "I don't think you should make a big deal out of this right now."

"He came back from the dead," Molly argued. "If I can't make a big deal about that, what can I make a big deal about?"

"Me," Zander answered automatically as Quinn's eyes swept the room, not stopping until they landed on Harper. "I'm a big deal. Hey, Quinn. I can't tell you how excited I am to see you. Are you just dropping by to see the new business space? Nice, isn't it?"

Quinn nodded, although he never moved his gaze from Harper's face. "It's great."

"Do you want to see the storage room?" Zander asked pointedly.

"Actually, I came by to see Harper," Quinn answered. "It's a nice day out, better than the past few days. I thought maybe we could take a walk ... and talk."

"Harper has work to do," Zander supplied. "If you want to make an appointment for after Thanksgiving, though, I can have Molly look at our schedule."

"Don't listen to him," Harper said, waving in Zander's direction as she offered Quinn a shy smile. "I think a walk sounds great. Let me grab my coat."

"Cool." Quinn beamed at her. "I don't want to take up much of your time, but I think we should touch base."

"I definitely agree." Harper snagged Zander's gaze as she slipped into her coat. "Zander can hold down the fort here. It will be totally fine."

And just like that, Zander realized he was cut out of the walk. The realization didn't brighten his mood one bit.

"WHAT ARE WE LOOKING AT?"

Jared was confused as Ned Patterson held up a large leather purse.

"I found this in the trunk," Ned explained, releasing the bag to Jared before sitting behind an ancient metal desk located in the corner of his office. "I thought it was strange since you guys took another purse from the scene before releasing the vehicle to me."

"Huh." Jared glanced at Mel. "He's right. We did take a purse from the front seat of the car. Vicky Thompson took it to the hospital with her."

"I don't remember Daniel mentioning her purse, do you?" Mel's confusion was evident as he rubbed the back of his neck. "That should've been turned over with her other belongings, but I didn't see it in the box the nurse delivered before we left."

"I didn't see it either. That means it wasn't in the room, right?"

"That means I need to call Daniel and figure out what happened to it," Mel corrected. "There's always the possibility that it was locked away in a safe or locker and they forgot about it."

"That's not likely, though."

"Definitely not." Mel pursed his lips as he joined his partner and glanced inside the purse. "Is there anything interesting in there?"

"As a matter of fact, there is," Ned replied. "There's a driver's license, credit cards, and even a library card with another name on it."

Jared stilled. "Another name? Like a man's name?"

"No, like a woman's name. Judy Lange. I ran her information through my database to see what I could come up with, because I thought maybe Judy was an aunt or mother or something. Then I saw the age and photo on the license, and realized Judy and Vicky were the same person. I thought there was a chance that Vicky had a twin or something, but not according to the records I found."

"What kind of records are you privy to?" Jared asked, curious despite himself. "You're not authorized for law enforcement record searches."

"No, but he is authorized to run driving records," Mel volunteered. "He can run license plates and licenses. Certain things pop in those searches, including open warrants."

"That's exactly what piqued my interest," Ned confirmed. "It seems Judy Lange is wanted in at least six states, and she has charges pending in all of them."

"For what?"

"I can't be sure, but I saw the word 'larceny' a few times. If you ask me, your dead woman was a grifter. She moved from state to state, probably passing bad checks and stealing from people. You'll have to track that part down, though. That's beyond my area of expertise."

Jared was legitimately stunned. "Well, I didn't see that coming."

"No, but it's another place to look," Mel said. "Perhaps there is motive for murder here after all."

ZANDER PACED THE INSIDE of GHI for what felt like forever once Harper disappeared from the building. In real time it was more like thirty seconds.

"I cannot believe she just wandered off with him," Zander complained, scuffing his feet against the linoleum floor. "What is she thinking?"

Molly took on a dreamy expression. "I think it's romantic."

"Yes, I'm sure Jared feels the same way," Zander snapped.

Molly had the grace to look abashed. "I didn't mean it that way. It's just ... the story is so amazing. He had amnesia and found his way back to her, for crying out loud. How can you not be swooning over this?"

"Because I'm a realist."

Eric snorted. "I think it's more apt to say that Zander understands that this story has more holes than Swiss cheese. He doesn't want Harper to get in trouble, and that's why he's worried."

"No, I've always disliked Quinn," Zander countered. "He's a tool. He thinks too highly of himself and he never put Harper's needs ahead of his own back when they were dating. As much as Jared irritates me — and he does — he always makes Harper's needs the priority. He would never purposely hurt her."

Eric tilted his head, considering. "Do you think Quinn would hurt her?"

"Probably not, but I can't be sure. He could be evil for all we know. He's hasn't been around for years."

"Then maybe Harper shouldn't be out there walking around with him," Eric suggested. "It might not be safe."

Molly rolled her eyes. "It's the middle of the day. They're walking around town. I'm sure they're fine."

"I'm going to make sure they're fine." Zander grabbed his coat from the back of his desk chair. "Eric is right. Harper needs to be watched. She's still in shock from Quinn's return. She doesn't understand what's really going on."

"And what's going on?" Molly challenged. "As far as I can tell, all this guy wants is to talk to her. Shame on him!" She wagged her finger for emphasis. "That clearly means he's evil."

"I can't even look at you." Zander turned on his heel. "You two hold down the fort. I'm going to save my best friend from evil. If you don't hear from me in an hour, assume Quinn killed me and ran off with my best friend. Call the National Guard if that happens."

Zander paused by the door, his hand on the bar. "Also, if that happens, I want a big statue erected in the town square honoring me for my sacrifice. I want it to say 'died for friendship' and make sure you get someone good at sculptures so I look hot."

Eric bit back a smirk. "We'll get right on that."

"Good. Don't let my sacrifice be in vain."

"Never."

NINE

With the new information backing them, Mel and Jared had no trouble tracking down Patty Lange, their victim's mother. She lived in one of those transitional homes for people of a certain age — she was only in her sixties but apparently needed help — and she was eating Jell-O and watching *Family Feud* when the police detectives knocked on her door.

"What did Judy do now?"

Patty asked the question the second Mel flashed his badge. She seemed resigned.

"Can we come in, Mrs. Lange?" Mel asked, his face immovable.

Patty glanced between the men for a beat before opening the door wider and taking a step back. "I'm not going to like this, am I?"

"Unfortunately, ma'am, I don't think so." Jared pressed his lips together in an approximation of a weak smile as he followed Patty to the small living room in her condominium unit. "Can we get you something to drink, ma'am?"

The look Patty shot Jared was full of suspicion ... and then defeat. It was as if she recognized the Whisper Cove police detectives were going to upend her life. "What happened?"

"Mrs. Lange, we regret to inform you that your daughter died in

Whisper Cove General Hospital yesterday," Mel volunteered, opting not to drag things out. "We're very sorry for your loss."

Patty clutched her hands together as she sank to the couch. "How?"

"We're trying to ascertain that, ma'am."

Patty's annoyance came out to play as she tugged on her limited patience. "You have no idea how my daughter turned up in the hospital, huh? Are you going to stick to that story? You're detectives. I saw your badges. You're here because you think Judy was murdered. There's no sense in denying it."

"We know she was murdered, ma'am." Jared chose his words carefully. "We're trying to figure out who had motive to carry out an attack on her."

"Well, if you're looking for people who want to hurt Judy, the list is long and sundry." Even though she was clearly upset, Patty held it together. "Why don't you start by telling me what happened, huh? After that, I don't know if I'll be any help, but I'll answer any questions you have."

"Of course." Mel launched into the tale. He kept things succinct, his voice calm, and never broke eye contact. "We didn't realize that Vicky Thompson wasn't a real person until we found the second purse in the trunk. Otherwise we would've notified you of her passing yesterday. We apologize."

Patty made a dismissive motion with her hands as she absorbed the words. "How could you have known? She had identification stating otherwise, right?"

"She did," Jared confirmed. "Since it was a single-car accident, though, we opted against issuing a ticket. She was banged up a bit after the rollover, a little frazzled, but we assumed she would be fine."

"How did someone get inside the hospital to poison her?" Patty asked.

"It's a small facility, only one duty nurse on each floor during the overnight hours," Mel explained. "Whoever it was waited until the nurse was doing her rounds and secluded around a corner so she couldn't see Judy's room."

"It sounds like it was well planned." Patty tapped her bottom lip.

"I'm sure you ran my daughter's real name when you found the second purse and discovered she's been ... um ... busy."

"We noticed she was active in the area when she was younger," Jared confirmed. "We also noted she had outstanding arrest warrants in multiple states."

Patty's eyebrows winged up. "Are you kidding? I didn't know that."

"I'm afraid we're not kidding," Mel replied. "She had quite the colorful reputation. Everything we managed to pull shows that she was ... a unique individual."

Patty barked out a laugh, but the sound was wan and utterly humorless. "You don't have to sugarcoat things for me, or walk on eggshells. I'm well aware of the type of person my daughter was. She learned it from her father. He was a grifter, too."

"She was still your daughter," Jared pointed out. "You obviously loved her."

"I *did* love her," Patty confirmed, taking on a far-off expression. "I was a terrible mother, though. I didn't have the energy to give her the attention she wanted. I have Lupus, you see, and that made me chronically tired when she was a kid. I couldn't keep up, and she was needy and desperate for attention.

"As she got older, she started looking for that attention from other people," she continued. "Her father was a loser to the hundredth degree, and he spent all of her childhood in and out of jail. It was mostly county lockup stuff, petty and ridiculous thievery, but whenever he would get out he would come around looking for money.

"Because Judy didn't think I was giving her the attention she deserved, she loved it when her father deigned to visit because he doted on her," she said. "He made a big show of pretending she was the center of his world ... and then he asked her to go through my purse and steal money for him."

Jared's stomach twisted at Patty's matter-of-fact delivery. "I'm sorry."

"I knew when she was a teenager that she was going to be trouble," Patty said. "I wanted to help her, make things better, but it was already too late. Patty was set on her future path. She didn't believe in work, always wanted something for nothing. I'm going to guarantee that almost every warrant that's been issued for her had something to do with bilking people out of money."

"Pretty much," Mel confirmed. "May I ask what she was doing here? According to the information we found in her file, she hadn't been in the area for at least ten years. Or, well, at least arrested in this area."

"Not so much as a visit," Patty confirmed. "She showed up out of nowhere about two weeks ago. It might have been three. I apologize. My days run together in this place."

"That's okay." Jared offered a charming smile. "Just tell us what you remember."

"She showed up out of the blue, acted like it hadn't been a decade since I last saw her, and wanted to chat about a few things," Patty responded. "The thing is, I knew the second I saw her that she was running on fumes. She seemed tired, stretched. She didn't want to admit that, though, and she made up grand stories about doing great and all these investment opportunities she had going."

"She wanted you to give her money," Mel surmised.

Patty bobbed her head. "She did. She wasn't happy when I explained I didn't have any money to give. The bulk of my disability and Social Security goes to this place. I pay for my room and then we make shopping lists, and the facility has people pick up those items for us. I don't have a lot left over at the end of the month."

"Did that upset Judy?"

"Yes, but she did her best to cover for it," Patty replied. "She made a big show of saying she was going to get a house we could both live in and make amends for past wrongs, but I knew she was blowing smoke. Besides that, I can't leave this place. They keep my medication regulated and I'm not always clear enough to do that myself. I could've never trusted Judy to pick up the slack, not on something that important."

"Do you have any idea who your daughter was currently working with?" Mel queried. "She must've had ties to someone in the area."

"I'm sure she did. She didn't tell me, though. You'll have to pull her police reports for lists of victims and associates. I honestly can't remember. She made a lot of enemies, some who visited my house looking for her at times. You're probably going to spend a lot of time chasing these people down."

"Well, we'll do our best." Jared awkwardly patted the woman's wrist. "We'll find answers for you."

"Thank you." Patty smiled, but it didn't make it all the way to her eyes. "I appreciate you guys being so diligent. Most people would ignore what happened to Judy because of her history. She'd be a throwaway to them."

"We're not most people. We'll be in touch."

HARPER WAS QUIET as she matched Quinn's pace, the brisk air turning her cheeks pink as the duo made their way to the beachfront property where they previously spent a lot of time together.

"Don't you want to say something?" Quinn asked finally, breaking the silence. "You haven't said a word in five minutes."

"I don't know what to say," Harper admitted, her smile rueful. "It's just so ... surreal."

"It is," Quinn agreed, leaning against a large rock and folding his arms over his chest. "We've talked about me. I monopolized the entire conversation yesterday, and then I got dragged away before I could ask about you."

Harper widened her eyes. "You want to talk about me? My life is ridiculously boring."

"I don't believe that."

"It's true."

"I still want to hear about it," Quinn said gently. "It must have been difficult for you when I disappeared."

Harper swallowed hard as she stared into his eyes. They were familiar, and yet different. It was a weird dichotomy. "I thought you were dead."

"Technically I am dead. It's going to be difficult convincing the government I'm not if I expect to reclaim my Social Security number and bank accounts."

"The accident was ... bad," Harper volunteered. "I went out to the scene once Mel called Zander to tell us what they found. At first, they were hopeful you would be found. They figured you couldn't have gone far. Although ... ." She trailed off.

"They thought they would find a body," Quinn supplied. "They told you I was dead and you believed them."

"It's not just that," Harper offered hurriedly. "Blood was found at the scene. A lot of blood."

"That must have been from the chest injury." Quinn absently touched the spot where his scar rested. "I wonder how it happened."

"I honestly don't know." Harper was earnest. "Mel warned me that the amount of blood you lost was enough to make you weak. If you passed out and your wounds weren't treated, well, the odds of survival weren't good.

"Still, for the first few hours at least, I was hopeful," she continued. "The state police brought in dogs. They found your scent and followed it to the woods. Somehow, though, they lost the trail and you disappeared.

"I remember being lost when I returned to my apartment that night," she said, her expression cloudy due to dark memories. "I was upset at the thought of you being out there alone. Zander was waiting for me, though, and he refused to leave me even though I wanted to wallow."

"You didn't want to wallow," Quinn countered. "You wanted to sneak back out to the woods to look for me yourself. No, don't bother denying it. Zander recognized your plan and refused to let you go. That was smart of him."

"I might have found you, though."

"We'll never know that," Quinn said. "There's no way of knowing where I was at that point. I can't remember. I wish I could, at least to give you peace of mind, but I can't."

"Yeah." Harper licked her lips as she regarded him, a wave of amazement washing over her. "I can't believe you're here. I honestly spent so much time looking for you that I lost track of myself for a bit. Zander pulled me back from the precipice, ordered me to stop searching the woods every single day, and then insisted we move in together.

"Those first few months, I was kind of like a zombie," she continued. "I gave up thinking we would find you alive a few days into things. I never stopped looking for your ghost, though. Not really."

"Oh." Realization washed over Quinn's features. "You wanted to put me to rest."

"I couldn't stand the idea of you wandering around the woods, lost, and never finding peace."

"Well, now I'm sad." Quinn's lips curved as he sheepishly shook his head. "I don't like the idea of you searching for a ghost that didn't exist."

"I guess we both have a few issues, huh?" Harper giggled as she dragged a hand through her shoulder-length hair. "I can't believe everything that has happened in such a short amount of time. It's so weird that you're here now. In some ways, it's as if no time has passed."

"Oh, now, that's not the world we live in," Quinn chided, shifting from one foot to the other. "We've lost years. There's no going back."

"Definitely not," Harper agreed readily. "I wouldn't want to go back, not even if it could save both of us some heartbreak. The fact that you're here is a miracle. I can't ask for more than that."

"Me either." Quinn instinctively reached out his fingers, as if he was going to touch Harper's face, but he let his hand drop when he saw the surprise register on her features. "Sorry. Old habit."

"Yeah, well ... ." Harper was clearly uncomfortable. "You know I'm with Jared, right?" She felt stupid asking the question. It was only now, under the bright light of day, that she realized how jumbled things got the previous afternoon. Emotions and greetings overlapped to the point where she could barely remember what came out publicly ... and what didn't.

"I know you're with the police officer who dragged me down to the station for questioning yesterday," Quinn said dryly. "I saw the way you interacted when he showed up. You instantly went to him, and he's been a little ... territorial ... with me."

Harper couldn't hide her surprise. "Jared doesn't get territorial."

"Probably not in front of you," Quinn conceded. "When it's just the boys, though, he has to mark his territory."

For some reason — and Harper recognized the comment was made in jest and yet she couldn't separate herself from the momentary jolt of annoyance coursing through her — the blond ghost hunter didn't like Quinn's tone.

"Jared is doing his job," Harper argued. "When you disappeared, it was a big deal. You were all over the news cycles and people brought search dogs from other states to help. It was a media circus."

Quinn held up his hands in a placating manner. "I didn't mean to upset you."

"You didn't upset me," Harper lied. "It's just ... Jared is a good man. He had no choice but to question you."

"He came back this morning to question me a second time," Quinn volunteered. "He thinks I had something to do with some woman dying after an accident or something."

The admission caught Harper off guard. "Vicky Thompson? The woman from the rollover accident."

Quinn nodded. "I was there the day of the accident. I hadn't yet worked up the courage to visit you, so I thought heading back out to the scene might jog my memory. I saw what happened and ran over to help, but once the woman was safely out of her vehicle I started to panic."

"How come?"

"Because the only Whisper Cove police officer I ever knew was Mel," Quinn answered. "I knew the second I saw him, he would recognize me. I didn't have a problem answering questions, mind you, but I wanted to see you before that was necessary. It only seemed fair that I would be the one to break the news to you."

"So you left the scene of an accident?"

"I panicked. It was a terrible decision. I don't know what I was thinking."

"I don't either," Harper hedged. "Was Jared mad when he visited you?"

"We had breakfast together actually." Quinn turned rueful. "He seemed nice enough, maybe a little tired. He clearly had a lot on his mind."

"We don't get a lot of murders in Whisper Cove."

Quinn's lips curved, reflecting genuine amusement. "I wasn't talking about that. I was talking about my return. It can't be easy for him. I mean ... we were together at the time of my disappearance. He probably can't help himself from worrying that you'll be torn between us or something."

Instead of reacting with earnest emotion, Harper barked out a laugh. "Oh, don't be ridiculous." Her mirth bubbled up. "Jared knows he has absolutely nothing to worry about. He's not the sort of guy to dwell on things like that. Don't even get yourself worked up about it. Jared is fine."

Quinn searched Harper's face for a long beat, his expression unreadable. "So ... you're happy, huh?"

Harper realized her reaction could be misconstrued as dismissive after the fact and quickly collected herself. "I didn't mean that the way it sounded. It's just ... Jared and I have been through a lot. There's nothing that can separate us."

"Not even a back-from-the-dead boyfriend, huh?"

"No." Harper opted for honesty. "I don't mean that to hurt you, but it's been a long time. I'm not the same person you dated years ago. I'm more sure of myself now, strong. Jared and I fit together. I'll always be fond of you because you're part of my past but ... it was a different time."

"Right." Quinn pressed his lips together. "Just tell me you're happy."

"I *am* happy. I love Jared with my whole heart."

"And he loves you?"

Harper mustered a girly smile, one that made her look impossibly young. "He does. I never doubt that."

"Well, that's great."

Harper took sympathy on him. "He's a good man. I think you would really like him … under different circumstances."

"When he's not questioning me for murder, right?"

"That's a given."

Despite himself, Quinn chuckled. "You're right about being different. You're still the same in a lot of ways, though." He opened his arms in offering. "We were friends before we started dating. I would like to be friends again. I don't want to go back to a place where you don't exist in my world."

Harper's smile was wide and heartfelt as she stepped into his embrace. "I don't want to go back to that place either."

From across the street, Zander watched the exchange, a huge ball of worry coiling in his stomach. He didn't trust Quinn — it was obvious he had an agenda — and apparently Harper was walking right into his net.

No, Zander didn't like the turn of events one bit. He had no idea how to fix things, though. He was truly at a loss.

TEN

Bone tired, Jared sighed with relief when he slipped off his shoes and coat by the front door and tilted his head to listen for the telltale sounds of Harper and Zander going about daily life. It was well after six before he returned to the house. He texted Harper to eat without him because he had no idea when he would finish his shift. He assumed that meant she would dine with Zander, but he was mildly worried about the silence that greeted him.

"It's about time you got here," Zander snapped as he walked into the room and came face to face with Jared. "I'm about to have a meltdown."

"I thought that was your perpetual state," Jared said dryly as he threw himself on the couch and rested his feet on the coffee table. "Where is Harper?"

"Oh, like you care."

Jared narrowed his eyes to dangerous slits. "You don't want to go there. Now, I'll repeat my question. Where is Harper?"

Perhaps sensing that Jared wasn't in the mood to be trifled with, Zander adjusted his tone. "We ordered Chinese. She's picking it up with Shawn."

"Oh." Jared furrowed his brow. "I thought you guys already ate."

"She refused to eat without you."

The statement, although minor, bolstered Jared's spirits a bit. "That was nice of her."

"No, it was nice of me," Zander countered. "I'm starving, running on fumes. You have no idea the day I've had." He dramatically threw himself in the chair at the edge of the room. "I need a spa day after what I've gone through."

"And what have you gone through?"

"Um ... what do you think?"

Jared blinked several times in rapid succession. "I have no idea. That's why I asked."

"Oh." Zander straightened. "Didn't Harper tell you how we spent our day?"

"No, I was busy with work. I assumed you guys were at the office."

"Oh, we were at the office."

Jared's anxiety ticked up a notch. "Zander, my day has been terrible. I found out my victim was a grifter and any number of people could've wanted her dead and then I had to inform her mother she was dead. That's on top of going to the morgue and looking at a body. So, I'm sure you understand, I'm in no mood to mess around."

"Okay. Geez." Zander held up his hands and shook them. "I didn't have an easy day either. There's no reason to get all worked up."

"Just tell me what happened."

"Fine." Zander shifted on his chair to get comfortable. "We had a visit from an old friend ... and it went on and on and on."

Jared expected the news. There was no way Quinn would come back to town and hide in his hotel room all day. Still, it grated knowing that the man — an individual he didn't trust — spent the better part of the day with the woman he loved. He was glad he heard the news when Harper wasn't around to witness his reaction. "I see."

Zander cocked an eyebrow. "You see? That's all you have to say?"

"I'm collecting my thoughts."

Even though he was often self-absorbed and eager to irritate Jared, Zander took pity on the man. He could see the emotional upheaval in the police detective's eyes and he could only imagine the worry that plagued him because of Quinn's miraculous resurrection.

"He didn't hurt her or anything," Zander offered quickly. "He showed up at the office and asked her to go for a walk so they could talk. She agreed. They didn't go far, down to the beach, and they talked for a long time."

"Did they look ... happy?"

The question caught Zander off guard. "I don't think that's the word I would use," he hedged once he had time to reflect on how to answer. "They looked intense, as if they were having an important conversation, and then they hugged."

"They hugged?" It took everything Jared had to keep from blowing up at the news.

"It wasn't a sexy hug. It was an 'I'm glad you didn't really suffer and die in the woods' hug. I don't know what they said to each other because I was spying across the road, but I'm certain it wasn't like that. There was no petting or anything."

"Okay, well ... that's good. I mean ... I guess that's good." Jared found himself in the awkward position of not knowing what to do with his hands. Ultimately, he decided to rub them against his jeans. "I'm glad it wasn't a romantic rendezvous."

"Harper would never do that." Zander's voice was shrill. "You should know that."

"I *do* know that."

"So ... why are you so worked up?"

"Because I love her, and I feel as if I'm trapped in a situation where I can't react the way I want to react," Jared replied without hesitation. "I want to grab that guy by the back of his neck and shake him until answers I believe start falling out. I can't do that, though, because this is Harper's situation to deal with."

"You're part of the situation, too," Zander pointed out. "You have a right to feel what you're feeling."

"I don't want to hurt Harper."

"So, instead you're going to eat your feelings?" Zander challenged. "That doesn't sound very healthy."

"I don't have a roadmap for this. I'm doing the best I can."

"I get that." Zander leaned forward so Jared had no choice but to meet his gaze. "You have to tell her how you feel, though. She needs to know."

"I will tell her how I feel ... once I know that the situation has calmed a bit. She needs time to adjust."

"And you don't want to rock the boat," Zander surmised. "I get it. That doesn't change the fact that Quinn Jackson is up to something, and it can't possibly be good. In fact, I'm betting that he's evil incarnate and he's trying to take over Whisper Cove for some nefarious plan."

The words escaped Zander's mouth at the exact moment the front door of the house opened to allow Harper and Shawn entrance. Harper pulled up short and stared hard at her friend as Shawn skirted around her, his arms laden with Chinese takeout.

"What did you just say?" Harper asked finally, when it became clear Zander wasn't going to continue on his diatribe without prodding.

Uncomfortable, Zander shifted on his chair and licked his lips. "I was just talking to Jared about a television show I watched a few days ago."

"Oh, really?" Harper shrugged out of her coat. "What was it about?"

"A woman who hadn't seen her ex-boyfriend for six years because she thought he was dead but believed every ridiculous word that came out of his mouth upon his return even though it made no sense," Zander replied, unruffled. "Right up until the moment he stole her money and tried to kill her, she believed he was just an old friend who had something horrible happen to him."

"Wow." Harper faked an enthusiastic thumbs-up. "What are the odds that story would air right before Quinn showed up? I mean ... that's freaky."

Sensing a potential war, Jared pressed the heel of his hand to his forehead as he straightened. "Hey, Heart. Why don't you come over here with me, huh?"

Harper ignored the request and continued glaring at Zander. "I don't understand why you're being like this. First you follow us on our walk — yes, we knew you were there spying — and then you spend the entire afternoon getting in passive aggressive digs when Quinn is hanging around the office. I don't get it."

Jared's stomach flipped. "He spent the whole day with you?"

"Is that a problem?" Harper asked pointedly. "He wanted to see GHI, what we do. When he disappeared, we didn't have the office space we do now. Eric and Molly weren't with us either. It was a vastly different operation."

"Oh, please." Zander rolled his eyes. "It was the exact same operation, except now there are four of us to insult one another when things get hairy. He wasn't hanging around because he wanted to see the operation. He was hanging around because he wanted to be close to you. I'm not an idiot."

"You sound like an idiot."

"Let's not fight," Shawn interjected worriedly. As the newest member of their little foursome, he was the most uncomfortable when the insults started to fly. "We got crab rangoon and entrees for everybody. Who doesn't love crab rangoon?"

Zander pretended he hadn't heard his boyfriend's plea. "Harp, you know I love you ... ."

"Don't finish that sentence," Harper warned, jabbing a finger in Zander's direction. "You're going to add a 'but' on there. Nobody wants to hear that 'but.'"

Technically, Jared was more than willing to listen to the "but." He didn't want to be painted as the bad guy in this scenario, though, so he calmly kept his mouth shut.

"I'm trying to protect you, Harper," Zander snapped, his temper on full display. "You refuse to see what's right in front of you. This is like when Quinn disappeared all over again. Who was the one who handled things back then? I know you like to pretend that you're the one who handles things best, but I was the one who kept you together back then."

"You were," Harper admitted, her eyes flashing with annoyance. "You saved me. I saved myself after that. I pulled myself together. I think I've done a pretty good job living my life since then. Obviously you feel differently."

"I didn't say that," Zander grumbled. "You're my best friend. I want to protect you. That's allowed."

"Quinn doesn't want to hurt me, though, so what are you protecting me from?"

"Him." Zander didn't back down. "He's not a good man. He never was."

"You're worrying about nothing," Harper countered. "Everything is going to be perfectly fine. I guarantee it."

Zander remained dubious. "You can't see him for what he is. I can. Don't trust him."

"It's going to be fine." Harper waved off Zander's concern as if he'd told her the color she picked for her sweater that day washed her out. "Nothing bad is going to happen. Trust me."

JARED WAS MORE THAN ready for bed when it came time to turn in. He'd already stripped down to his boxers by the time Harper strolled out of the bathroom. She took a moment to watch him, her heart rolling when she saw the misery lining his face.

"Are you okay?"

Jared hadn't realized she was watching and he forced a smile to cover his worry. "Of course. I was just thinking about some of the stuff we discovered about Judy Lange."

"Yeah, that was weird," Harper agreed, moving to sit at the end of the bed with him. She was dressed in a plain T-shirt and nothing else. "I don't think that's what has you worried, though."

"Oh, yeah? What do you think has me worried?"

Harper saw no reason to lie. "Quinn. You're worried about Quinn, too, aren't you?"

"What would make you say that?"

Harper allowed a hint of anger to creep into her tone. "Answering a question with a question is a deflection. You taught me that."

"Actually, you already knew that when we met." Jared's smile was rueful. "I believe you said exactly that to me not long after our first interaction, when I was trying to deflect a question because it made me uncomfortable."

"So, why are you doing the same now?"

Jared held out his hands and shrugged. "I don't know, Heart. I'm out of my element in this situation and I have no idea what to do. It's ... frustrating."

Instead of reacting with anger, Harper was calm as she collected Jared's hands between hers and asked the obvious question. "What's wrong?"

"I'm afraid." Jared hadn't meant to blurt it out, but when confronted at the moment, he could do nothing but tell the truth. "I'm so afraid that you're going to decide that you belong with Quinn — that it's somehow kismet that he returned — that I think I'm going to make myself sick."

The heartfelt admission was enough to cause Harper to gasp. "You can't think that."

"I don't want to think that. I can't stop myself from worrying, though. This situation is ... like nothing I've ever had to deal with before."

"I don't think most people ever have to deal with situations like this," Harper admitted, searching for the correct words to soothe Jared's obviously frazzled nerves. "You know I love you, right?"

"I love you, too."

"I don't doubt that. I never doubt that. You're apparently the one doubting that."

"It's not that I doubt that," Jared protested, hating how petulant he sounded. "It's just ... your ex-boyfriend is back. He came back from the dead. We're only together because you're no longer with him. I can't help feeling vulnerable ... although I don't even know if that's the right word."

"Jared, I know this is difficult, and I don't think I've been very sympathetic to your feelings since it started." Harper searched for the right words. "I didn't take your feelings into consideration. I simply assumed you would understand how I feel about the situation, but that's not possible because you're not psychic."

"No, I'm not psychic." He swallowed hard. "How do you feel?"

"Mildly overwhelmed," she answered without hesitation. "When I first saw him, I thought it was a dream. I didn't know what to think or feel. The one thing I can tell you with absolute certainty that I did not feel, however, was love. I didn't look at him and fall back in love all over again. In fact ... ." Harper trailed off, unsure if what she was about to say sounded mean.

"Keep going," Jared prodded. "I like what you're saying so far."

Despite the serious nature of the conversation, Harper chuckled. "I bet you do. I was just going to say that I don't think I ever loved Quinn."

"No?" Jared kept his voice deceptively mild. "I wasn't sure how you felt."

"I think I convinced myself that I loved him back then, but what I felt at the time pales in comparison with what I feel for you now. I don't think it could've possibly been love."

Even though he knew it was ridiculous, Jared wanted to pull her on his lap and weep until the fear finished seeping out of his soul. "I love you so much that I can't help but worry about your former boyfriend coming back. I hate it. I'm not an insecure person. I've never felt insecure where you're concerned before. I can't help it now, though, and I'm sorry."

"Oh, don't be sorry." Harper shifted so she could face him and ran her fingers over his face. It was a simple gesture, nothing romantic about it, and yet it was wildly passionate all the same. It was a statement of belonging without words. Harper knew Jared needed to hear the words this go-around, too. "You don't have anything to worry about. I only want to be with you. It never occurred to me you didn't know that, and I'm so sorry."

"You don't have to apologize. You haven't done anything wrong."

"No, I guess I haven't," Harper agreed. "I should've thought about your feelings, though. If our positions were reversed and you had a former girlfriend come back from the dead, I would be worried, too. I wouldn't be able to help myself. I would need reassurance, and that's something I didn't provide for you."

"I don't want to need reassurance." Jared was firm. "I like that neither of us needs it on a regular basis. It's just ... I don't know what to do, or how to feel. This whole thing has thrown me for a loop and I'm so afraid that I'm going to say or do the wrong thing."

"What's the wrong thing?"

Jared held his hands palms out. "I don't know. I'll say it, though. I just know it."

"You won't. There is no wrong thing. You simply need to feel what you feel. I don't want you to pretend to feel otherwise because that's not real and you and I, above everything else, are always real."

"We are." Jared choked back a sob when she slipped into his arms and wrapped herself around him. "I really am sorry. You shouldn't have to deal with this on top of everything else."

"I'm okay dealing with this. You shouldn't have to deal with this either."

"The world isn't always fair," Jared said philosophically, causing Harper to chuckle. "We'll deal with this like we do anything else."

"Together?"

Jared nodded. "That's the plan."

"It's a good plan." She pressed a firm kiss to the corner of his mouth. "It's okay if you're off your game. I am, too. There is no roadmap for what we're dealing with. We're going to have to draw our own map."

"As long as you're safe ... and with me ... I don't need a map."

"Well, I'm both." Harper gave him a searching gaze. "I was going to bug you to give me some insight on why you're questioning Quinn about helping the woman out of her car at the accident site, but I think that can wait until tomorrow. For the rest of tonight, how about we spend some quiet time, just the two of us?"

Jared rested his forehead against hers and smiled. "I think that's the best offer I've had all day."

"That goes for both of us."

ELEVEN

J ared woke in his favorite position. He was on his back, naked, and Harper was sleeping with her head on his chest. His arm was wrapped snugly around her slim back, and he was of the mind that nothing was better than a morning spent exactly like this.

Things only got better when Harper stirred.

"Morning." She was something of a slow starter, always taking time to stretch and snuggle close rather than immediately hop out of bed. Jared had no complaints, because this was the most relaxed he'd felt since Quinn Jackson turned back up in their lives.

"Good morning, Heart." Jared gave her a soft kiss. "How did you sleep?"

"Hard. How did you sleep?"

"Good." It was the truth. Unlike the previous evening, Jared was down for the count the moment his head hit the pillow. "I felt you next to me the entire night, so it was nice."

"Aren't I next to you every night?"

"Yeah. I like it, though."

"I like it, too." Harper propped herself on an elbow and rested her hand on his bare chest as she studied him. "Are you feeling better about everything else?"

Thanks to the bright sunshine filtering through the window, Jared's reddening cheeks were on full display. "I'm sorry about that. I shouldn't have let it get to me."

"You have a right to be upset. I should've taken your feelings into consideration. It's just ... I love you so much. It never occurred to me that you wouldn't magically know that."

"I did know it. I simply needed to be reminded of it."

"Well, consider yourself reminded." Harper smacked a loud kiss against the corner of his mouth at the same moment his stomach elicited a rather exaggerated growl. "Wow. Someone is hungry."

"I worked up an appetite last night."

"Who didn't?" Harper's grin was bright and lazy. "How does a quick shower — together, of course — sound? I figure, by the time we're done, Zander will have breakfast ready."

"How do you know Zander is cooking breakfast?"

"He'll want to make up for our fight last night."

"You didn't really allow him to turn it into a fight. You kind of cut him off at the knees."

"That's because he's being ridiculous."

As much as he didn't want to fight, Jared felt the need to stand up for Zander. "He's worried about you. Maybe not for the same reasons I am, but he's worried all the same. He shouldn't be penalized for that."

Harper widened her eyes to saucer-like proportions. "Since when are you standing up for Zander?"

"Since I understand a bit of what he's feeling. I know you want to believe Quinn because the alternative is something you simply don't want to deal with, but I don't know that I believe his motivations are as altruistic as he pretends."

Instead of snapping, or offering words that would start a fight, Harper merely cocked her head. "I'm assuming you have a reason for thinking this."

"Several."

"Then I want to hear them." Harper gave him another kiss before rolling away. "After we've showered, though. I'm hungry, too. We'll talk about it over breakfast. For now, let's spend a little quality time together in the shower."

Jared's smile was so wide it almost split his entire face. "That's always the perfect way to start the day in my book."

"I happen to wholeheartedly agree."

"SO, WAIT ... QUINN HELPED that woman out of her car after she was in a serious accident and then left her by the side of the road to call for help on her own?" Shawn, his hair still mussed from sleep, sipped his coffee as Zander toiled behind the counter island.

Even though Harper was convinced Zander would want to play nice this morning, she found she was wrong. Her best friend was still holding a grudge, although it wasn't overtly on display for everyone to uncomfortably absorb.

"Basically," Jared confirmed.

"He told me about that," Harper protested. "He didn't hide it. He said he thought Mel would be the one called to the scene and that he wanted to see me before anyone else had the chance to break the news that he was alive. He said he panicked. I don't think he did a good thing, but it's hardly the end of the world."

"My problem with that is he only told you after I questioned him about it over breakfast," Jared argued, a mug of coffee clutched tightly in his hands. "I'm betting he didn't tell you about that."

"On the contrary. He did tell me about that. He said you guys had a decent if somewhat stressful conversation."

Jared's eyebrows migrated north. "He told you?"

"He did."

Jared rubbed his chin, considering. "I'm actually surprised he said anything. Maybe I was wrong about him."

"I don't think it's that you're wrong," Harper hedged. "I think it's that you're antsy because of the other stuff. You don't need to worry, though. I told you last night, you're the only one for me."

"You did tell me that," Jared agreed, lowering his forehead so he could rub his nose against hers. "I appreciate the sentiment and feel the same way."

"Oh, welcome to Barfsville," Zander intoned, rolling his eyes as he flipped hash browns with a spatula. "I'm so glad you guys are gooey and in love again — no, really, I was a little worried Jared would swallow his feelings for so long he would explode, but I'm no longer fearful that will happen — but I think you guys are missing the obvious problem here."

"What's the obvious problem?" Shawn asked.

"Quinn very clearly wants to play the victim," Zander replied. "He waited until right after Jared left his hotel to track us down, then he did his 'woe is me' whine to tug on Harper's heartstrings — and of course she can't turn her back because the dude was technically dead to us forty-eight hours ago — and then he decided to put her in a position where she would ultimately have to choose sides between him and Jared."

Harper balked. "He did not."

"No? I heard him talking to Eric when you were ordering sandwiches for lunch with Molly," Zander argued. "He wanted to know what Eric thought about Jared."

"I didn't hear that."

"You were busy deciding between roast beef and turkey. He wanted to know what Eric thought about Jared, whether he was good for you or not, and he couched it in a way that he was simply looking out for your best interests."

"That's kind of weird," Jared admitted after a beat. "He acted differently with me at the hotel. He said he wasn't interested in driving a wedge between us because he had something going on with a woman back in New York."

"He did?" Harper had no idea what to make of that particular tidbit. After a few moments of contemplation, she decided it was a good thing. "That's probably for the best. He's not here for me. He's here to make sure I'm okay and no longer wondering what happened to him. It's been years. Feelings change."

"Yes, but he's acting like a jealous boyfriend." Zander, in no mood to cede a fight, was like an angry dog with a bone. "He plays all nice and sweet in front of you, he tries to make Jared think he's not a threat, and then he acts all coy when questioning Eric. That's a pattern."

"I'm not sure I see the pattern," Shawn admitted. "To me, he sounds like a guy who is struggling to come to terms with a few things. I mean ... think about it. What if you were in an accident today and disappeared for five years? What if I stayed behind, mourned, and then moved on?

"Now, you could move to another city and find someone to date because you don't remember the life you've left behind, but that doesn't mean you wouldn't always feel something was missing," he continued. "Then, when those memories came back, the feelings did, too. The thing is, it's not normal feelings because time hasn't passed the same way for you.

"Sure, five years have passed, and you remember those five years, but when the past slaps you upside the head, all those emotions and memories are like a train that you can't outrun," he said. "Maybe Quinn is simply trying to come to grips with what he lost — including his mother — and he's not making the best decisions. I'm not sure any of us could say we would do better in the exact same situation."

"I agree with Shawn," Harper said. "I don't think Quinn is here to hurt anyone."

"There is one other thing I've yet to tell you," Jared noted. "I don't know if it will change your mind, but it gives me pause."

"Do I even want to know?"

"I want to know," Zander snapped. "Tell me what that evil freak has done now."

Harper bit back a sigh as she rubbed her forehead, earning a sympathetic look from Jared as he ran his hand over her back in a soothing manner.

"You never asked, so I didn't volunteer this information sooner, but there was a reason I came looking for you the day Quinn showed up."

Harper stilled, surprised. "Huh. I never even thought about that. You didn't have a reason to be out in the cornfield that day."

"Actually, I did." Jared sucked in a bracing breath. "When we were at the hospital investigating Judy Lange's death — this was when we still thought her name was Vicky Thompson — we watched video of the front door.

"The hospital doesn't have camera footage of every floor, which is too bad, because it would be saving us a lot of grief right about now," he continued. "They do over the front door, though, and one of the people who entered the building long after visiting hours were over was a man I didn't recognize ... but Mel did."

Zander snapped his fingers in a loud and aggressive manner. "Quinn!"

Jared nodded. "It was him, and he entered the hospital, stayed for about twenty-five minutes, and then left."

Harper was dumbfounded. "What did he say he was doing?"

"He said he was instructed to check in with the local hospital because his memory issues could cause headaches and stuff," Jared replied. "He said he was doing that."

"In the middle of the night?" Shawn, who had previously been on Quinn's side, was clearly waffling. "That doesn't make a lot of sense to me."

"It doesn't make sense to me either," Jared said. "I mean ... isn't that something you would do during the day? You know, when a doctor was actually at the hospital and available for a consultation."

Harper's bafflement was on full display. "I don't know what to say to that."

"I know what to say to it," Zander said without hesitation. "Clearly Quinn and Judy Lange were in cahoots."

Amused despite himself, Jared grinned over the rim of his coffee mug. "Cahoots? I don't believe I've heard that word in a very long time. I'm pretty sure the last time was during *Beverly Hillbillies* reruns."

"Oh, laugh if you must, but I know what I'm talking about," Zander drawled. "Quinn miraculously saved her from a car accident in the same place he supposedly died years ago? I don't believe it. Then he was at the hospital when she died. I bet they were doing something illegal."

"What?" Shawn asked, legitimately curious.

"I have no idea. Maybe they were plotting murders or selling drugs. Oh, maybe Quinn is forming his own prostitution ring."

"Yes, that sounds exactly like him," Harper said dryly.

"You don't really know him," Zander pointed out. "He's been gone from your life for a very long time. The last time you saw him, you were twenty-two years old. You were an idiot."

"Thank you, Zander."

"Hey, I was an idiot at that age, too. You were a kid, though. That's the point. You're an adult now. You're much smarter than you used to be. You should recognize he's up to something."

"I'm not sure I believe that," Harper hedged, risking a glance at Jared. "I'm willing to consider it, though. I promise I'll be careful. Heck, I'll even try to get some information out of him if he stops by again."

"Are you going to seek him out?" Jared asked. It was a pointed question, but he had to know.

"No." Harper shook her head, firm. "I don't want to hurt his feelings or anything, but now that I know the truth, I'm okay if he wants to leave and head back to his life in New York. We can email occasionally, keep up on each other's lives. I don't see our day-to-day activities overlapping, though."

"I'm happy to hear that."

"I figured you would be." Harper gave Jared a loud kiss before turning her head to the front door as the bell chimed. "Who would be visiting this early in the morning on a work day?"

"It's probably Quinn stopping by to be a total gentleman," Zander drawled.

"Or it's my mother coming by with more turkey directions," Harper shot back, slowly getting to her feet. "I'll get the door. You'd better have my breakfast ready when I get back. I can't hold out much longer."

"I'm not your slave," Zander called to her back.

"You're going to be the guy I wrestle down and tickle until he gives in and apologizes once Shawn and Jared leave for the day," Harper supplied. "You have that to look forward to."

Amused by the interaction, Jared pursed his lips as Zander stewed next to the stove. Equally delighted, Shawn watched his boyfriend mutter under his breath and curse a bevy of different people. The situation was so funny, Jared barely glanced at the door when Harper returned. He did a huge double take, though, when he realized she wasn't alone.

"Quinn," Jared said quickly, the knots between his shoulder blades immediately returning. "I didn't know you were stopping by this morning."

"I didn't know you were going to be here either," Quinn said, an air of innocence swirling around him. "I don't want to interrupt or anything, but I was up and saw the lights. I figured Harper wouldn't mind catching up a bit."

"You were up and noticed the lights on a street that only has two houses?" Zander challenged. "That sounds completely plausible."

Harper shot him a warning look. "It's perfectly fine," she said. "We're just hanging around this morning. I don't think we're going into the office. Jared and Shawn have to leave for work in a little bit, but Zander and I are going to be lazy."

"I'm not going to be lazy," Zander argued. "We have shopping to do for Thanksgiving. You can't be lazy when there's shopping to do."

Harper made a face. "We already did our shopping."

"We're not done. I told you we wouldn't be able to escape with only one trip."

"But ... what do we need? I double and triple checked our list."

"We need oysters, fresh bread chunks for stuffing, filling for blueberry pie ... and other stuff."

Harper was instantly suspicious. "Since when do we have blueberry pie for Thanksgiving?"

"Since Jared made a special request," Zander replied, not missing a beat.

Harper slowly slid her eyes to her boyfriend. "You made a special request for a blueberry pie, huh?"

He hadn't. Jared was a big fan of Zander's blueberry pie, but he was fine with pumpkin for the holiday. Still, since Zander was a master at irritating people and Quinn was high on his current list of enemies, Jared didn't want to alienate the man. "I did."

"See?" Zander sneered.

"Well, you don't need me for shopping," Harper said. "I can stay here with Quinn while you're handling the pre-holiday hordes."

Jared inserted himself into the conversation before he thought better about doing it. "I'm actually going to take the day off work, so we can all hang together."

Harper was beyond confused. "I'm sorry but ... what?"

"I'm hanging around the house," Jared repeated. "We have stuff to talk about for the move and I would love to spend quality time with Quinn so ... yeah, I'm hanging here for the day."

Quinn, clearly uncomfortable, shuffled from one foot to the other. "I feel as if I've interrupted something."

"You have," Zander said pointedly. "You should probably leave while we sort it out."

"Zander!" Harper was horrified by her friend's manners. "Don't talk to him that way."

"I'm not talking to him any particular way," Zander sniffed. "I'm merely stating a fact. We have a lot going on here. Now is not the best time for him to stop in unannounced."

Quinn read the obvious signals. "You're right. I shouldn't have stopped without calling first."

"I'm always right," Zander grumbled.

"I'll run out and handle my own errands for a bit, leave you guys to ... whatever it is you have planned for the day. I'll call you later, Harper. Maybe we can meet up for coffee or something."

Harper nodded, resigned. "That would be nice. I'm sorry about all of this."

"Don't worry about it." Quinn appeared eager to escape the house. "I'll ... um ... be in touch."

Harper waited for the sound of the front door closing before exploding. "What the heck was that?"

Jared and Zander adopted twin looks of innocence.

"I have no idea what you're talking about," Jared offered. "I was simply making plans for my day. Now, where is that breakfast? I don't have a lot of time before I have to get to work."

Harper wrinkled her forehead as she absorbed the change of plans. If she thought Jared was simply over the possibility of being displaced by Quinn — something that was absolutely ludicrous — she was sadly mistaken. Things were nowhere near being fixed, and wouldn't be as long as Quinn was a force in their lives.

"I'm hungry, too," she said finally. "I'm going to need my strength if I plan on surviving the grocery store this time of year."

"Definitely," Jared agreed. "You need to bulk up on the carbs. It's going to be a long day."

TWELVE

"**I** need the notes from the interview with Quinn Jackson."
Jared didn't bother greeting his partner when he walked into the office they shared, instead getting right to the heart of matters.

Mel slowly lifted his eyes and snagged his partner's gaze. "Are you sure that's a good idea?"

"Yes."

Mel waited for him to continue.

"I'm sure it's what I have to do," Jared clarified after a beat. "I don't buy his story ... and I don't particularly believe he's here for altruistic reasons."

"When did he say he was here for altruistic reasons?"

"You know what I mean."

"I do," Mel confirmed, bobbing his head. "You're upset because you think he's moving on your woman. I get that."

"If you think I'm doing this simply because I'm jealous ... ."

"I would be right," Mel finished.

"No, not completely right." Jared refused to back down. "I *am* worried he's here for Harper ... but not in the way you think."

Mel drew his eyebrows together and scratched at his chin. "Wait ... you think he wants to hurt her? That doesn't make a lot of sense to me. Why come back after years away and go after the girlfriend who has very clearly moved on?"

"I don't know." Jared edged his hip on the corner of his desk. "Maybe he didn't come back to town because of Harper at all. Maybe he came back for a different reason and she's simply collateral damage."

"What reason?"

"I don't know. I don't have an answer ... yet. Maybe he had ties to Judy Lange."

Whatever he was expecting, that wasn't it. Mel's eyebrows migrated north as he abandoned whatever he was looking at on his screen and focused entirely on Jared. "Are you kidding?"

"I don't often find murder funny."

"No, you don't," Mel agreed. "The thing is, why would Quinn have ties to Judy? It doesn't make any sense. Judy was a grifter who scammed money from people. I'm going to bet, when this all shakes out, that we find she had financial ties to whoever killed her."

"I've been thinking about that, and I have a problem with your theory," Jared said. "First off, Judy's mother didn't even know she was in the hospital. According to Patty, Judy only came back to the area because she was broke and wanted her mother to fund her lifestyle. I don't think she was here running a con."

"She stayed, though," Mel argued. "She must've had a reason for that. I'm guessing she found a partner of some sort. Even though we haven't followed up on the information Quinn provided, I'm going to guess that he hasn't maintained ties to this area during his absence."

"Why?"

"Because, if what you're saying is true and Quinn is lying about this amnesia thing, why would he maintain ties to an area where his true identity could be discovered? It's not just Harper and Zander who could ruin things for him. Most everyone in town either met him or became familiar with his image because photos were spread all over the news shows. He wasn't famous, but he had a recognizable face."

"I guess that's true." Even though he was loath to admit it, Jared had no choice but to concede that his partner had a point. "I simply find it hard to believe that Quinn just happened to be in the middle of nowhere when an accident occurred in the same spot he supposedly died years before."

"So ... what?" Mel was truly at a loss. "Do you think he was out there to fake Judy's death?"

"Maybe."

"Then why leave her behind to talk to us? What point is there to do anything of the sort? Nothing makes sense about that story."

Jared worked overtime to tamp down his agitation. "So, you believe him?"

"Regarding what?"

"He says he was out there to relive his past," Jared pressed. "Supposedly he visited the spot where Quinn Jackson ceased to be simply to see the accident site. That smells a little fishy to me."

"Uh-uh." Mel folded his arms over his chest. "That would mean he's the sentimental sort, right?"

"Yes."

"And men can't be sentimental, can they?"

"I didn't say that," Jared protested, annoyed. "I simply find it weird."

"I understand that." Mel's tone was entirely too rational, something that set Jared's teeth on edge. "Just one question, though."

"What?" Jared practically barked out the word.

"Whenever we go past the interrogation room, the one right around that corner over there, you always touch the chair at the far end."

"So?"

"So, that happens to be the chair Harper sat in the night you brought her in for questioning before you started dating," Mel noted. "You told me over beers a few weeks ago that you thought you fell in love with her at that exact moment, although you weren't ready to admit that so soon ... even to yourself.

"So, I've noticed over the past six months, that every single time you go into that interrogation room, you touch the chair Harper sat in when she was here," he continued. "It's like a little ritual you go through. If you were a hockey player, I would think it's your version of a playoff beard."

"That is ridiculous."

"No, it's sentimental," Mel corrected. "I think it's kind of cute, although I had no idea you were so superstitious."

"I'm not superstitious."

Mel remained silent, waiting.

"Fine." Jared blew out a frustrated sigh. "I don't want criminals sitting in her chair. Sue me."

Mel couldn't hold back his smile. "It's not her chair."

"It is in my head."

"Fair enough." The older police officer held up his hands in defeat. "There's nothing wrong with being sentimental. My question is, if you get that way about a chair, why doesn't it make sense for Quinn to go to the spot where his life irrevocably changed?"

"I don't know." It was rare for Jared to feel at a loss for words. "He bothers me. He went to her office yesterday to talk to her and ended up hanging out with the entire crew for the afternoon."

"And you're jealous because you want to spend more time with Eric and Molly?"

"No, I'm not jealous."

"So, what's the problem?"

"It's just ... he's always around." Jared recognized that he sounded whiny and attempted to adjust his tone. "He was at the office yesterday. He showed up at the house this morning. I made a total idiot of myself when he showed up, too. I said I wasn't going to work.

"I didn't come right out and say it because I didn't want to admit it, but Harper knew why I suddenly didn't want to leave the house," he continued. "Thankfully Zander was mean enough to Quinn that he didn't want to hang around and he took off. That allowed me to maintain the bare minimum of dignity and leave for work."

"Yes, Zander is lovely when it comes to being mean to people," Mel drawled. "He won trophies for it in middle school. As for Harper and Quinn, do you really think Harper is the type to cheat?"

"No. Absolutely not." Jared vehemently shook his head. "She and I had a very long talk last night. Things are good between us. Even before we talked, though, I never thought she would cheat on me."

"So, what's the problem? Are you worried that she might want to cheat on you with the old flame? If so, trust me, you're being an idiot. Harper loves you. She's so wrapped up in you that it's a little disgusting, especially to a guy who has known her since she was a small child."

Despite himself, Jared chuckled. "She doesn't want him. I know that. We're good ... other than the fact that I'm going to have to explain why I acted like a ninny this morning, of course. It's him that I'm worried about."

"What do you think he wants?"

"Her."

Mel studied the younger man for a long beat. "He said the exact opposite to you."

"Yes, well, Zander had a good point this morning."

"Oh, well, if you're taking Zander's word for something, you're worse off than I envisioned."

Jared ignored the dig. "Zander pointed out that Quinn was playing all of us in exactly the right way. Playing the sympathy card with Harper, playing the 'I'm not into her' card with me. All the while, he keeps hanging around."

"Technically, he has no choice but to hang around," Mel reminded him. "We told him he can't leave town until we okay it."

"I know but ... ."

"You're going to obsess about this no matter what," Mel surmised. "I get it. While I think you're being ridiculous, I actually don't blame you for feeling the way that you do. She's your girlfriend and you love her. Being protective comes with the territory."

"I simply feel that it's a good idea to start digging into Quinn's story."

"Then we'll do it." Mel was blasé as he turned back to his computer. "The information needs to be confirmed anyway. I don't see the harm in focusing on that today."

"I'm glad you agree."

"WHAT IS THAT?"

Harper stared at the gourd Zander held with overt disdain, the activity in the bustling produce section at their local store threatening to cause her head to implode.

"This is a ... squash thing," Zander said knowingly, clutching the oddly-shaped vegetable tighter. "We need it for our Thanksgiving preparations."

Harper wasn't convinced. "What are you going to cook with that? I thought we got the acorn squash for eating."

"We did."

"So ... what's that for?"

"Ambiance."

"Of course." Harper rolled her neck as she avoided a frazzled-looking woman collecting yams. "I should've realized that ambiance was high on your list."

"There's nothing wrong with ambiance." Zander's gaze was speculative as he watched Harper pick through the decorative gourds on display. "Do you want to tell me what's wrong?"

Harper snapped her head in his direction, the question catching her off guard. "What makes you think something is wrong?"

"Because you have your 'I'm having deep thoughts' face on," Zander replied without hesitation. "I love your face — you know that — but your deep thoughts face is my least favorite."

"I'm not having deep thoughts."

Zander tossed another gourd in the cart without breaking eye contact. Harper took it as a dare.

"I'm not having deep thoughts," she repeated, her temper fraying.

"Right, because you're always in such a foul mood when it comes to shopping for the holidays."

Harper stared and blinked for what felt like forever. Then, inexplicably, she shook her head and offered a lame chuckle. "You are a complete and total pain when you want to be. You know that, right?"

"I'm well aware," Zander agreed, resting his elbows on the cart handle. "What's wrong? I thought things were good between you and Jared. You seemed goofy and in love again this morning."

"We are in love." Harper moved away from the gourd and yam display because she sensed it was about to be overrun. "We talked last night, and I realized I wasn't doing right by him."

Zander balked. "You treat him better than me. You do right by him. I'm the one getting the shaft."

Harper rolled her eyes. "Not that. Also, I don't treat him better than you. Stop being a baby."

"How can you possibly think you're not doing right by him?"

"I meant with the Quinn thing," Harper clarified. "I never once considered how it would affect him. All I could think about was myself, how weird it was to see him, and how he felt so far removed from my life it was like talking to a stranger."

"We'll get back to that 'removed' part in a second because I'm officially intrigued by that," Zander said. "Regarding the other stuff, Jared should know you love him. You tell him every five seconds, so much so that I want to retch whenever I'm around you guys. I don't, of course, because I'm a gentleman. I want to, though."

It was impossible for Harper to hide her eye roll. "Yeah, yeah, yeah. I get it. You're the king of the world."

"Only our little corner of the world."

"We're talking about Jared and me, though," Harper pressed. "He was worked up because of Quinn's return and I didn't even see it."

"Because he thought you would take off with Quinn and leave him in the dust?"

"Which is ridiculous."

"Totally," Zander agreed. "I pretty much told him that. You didn't even love Quinn."

Harper pressed her lips together, her face burning. "You don't have to say that so loudly."

Zander glanced around, oblivious. "I didn't realize it was a secret. Everyone I know is aware of it, and that includes you."

"I'm aware." Her expression plaintive, Harper rubbed her hands together. "I told Jared the same thing. He was relieved. That's when I realized I should've given more consideration to his feelings."

"Hey, your former boyfriend came back from the dead," Zander drawled. "When Jared's former girlfriend comes back from the dead, then we'll talk about his feelings being more important than yours."

"He never said his feelings were more important than mine." Harper felt as if she were talking to a wall. "He was worried, though, and I feel bad about it. He should never worry about how I feel."

"If it's any consolation, I don't think he doubted your love. It was more that he worried you would be overwhelmed with feelings of responsibility where Quinn is concerned, since Quinn came first and all."

"I do feel a bit guilty about that," Harper hedged, chewing on her bottom lip. "Not guilty enough to do anything about it, mind you, but guilty all the same. He disappeared and I moved on as if nothing happened."

"No, you were frozen in time for months," Zander countered, his eyes traveling to the far side of the produce section where a lone man stood, back against the wall, and stared directly at them. "Do you know that guy?"

Harper followed her best friend's gaze and slowly shook her head. "No. Do you?"

"I can't say as I do, but he seems very intent on staring." Zander puffed out his chest and waved. The man, apparently embarrassed to be caught, turned his head and focused on the pie display. "Huh. That was sort of cute. His cheeks are turning red."

"You can't see his cheeks turning red from this far away," Harper protested.

"You don't know. I might be able to see it. I'm gifted in many ways."

"Yes, you're the gift that keeps on giving," Harper agreed. "Back to our conversation regarding Jared. I think he had a right to be upset. I thought long and hard about it last night. I wouldn't be happy if he had a former girlfriend pop up out of nowhere. I would like to think I would be gracious, but I'm not sure I have it in me. I think there might be some hair pulling."

Zander snorted, amusement rolling off him. "You're all talk. There's no way you would pull hair in public."

"I could pull some hair."

Tickled, Zander grabbed a container of caramel apples and dumped them in the cart. "There's a difference between those two scenarios. If one of Jared's ex-girlfriends showed up, it would be awkward for a different reason. She's an ex, after all. That's kind of stalkerish.

"As far as Quinn is concerned, you guys were still dating at the time of his disappearance," he continued. "Now, don't get me wrong, I don't think your relationship would've survived. His disappearance didn't allow for a natural conclusion, though. That's what worries Jared."

Realization dawned on Harper. "Oh, like he's worried that Quinn will want closure. Like maybe one more tumble for old time's sake."

Zander chuckled, his eyes going back to the man leaning against the wall, who just so happened to be watching them again. "Something like that."

"I'll just make sure Jared knows that's not going to happen."

"Uh-huh." Zander was thoughtful as he watched the man for signs he was up to something nefarious. "Do you think that guy is after you or me?"

Harper shrugged. "Why does it matter?"

"I have no idea. He's a little intense, though." Zander dug in his pocket for his phone and hit the camera app. "I wonder if he thinks he's flying under the radar. If so, he needs to take a chill pill."

Harper wrinkled her nose. "What are you doing?"

"Um ... filming him so I can show Shawn how desirable I am to other men."

Even though Harper knew she shouldn't be offended by the simple statement, she couldn't stop herself from bristling. "I think he's looking at me."

"You're dreaming," Zander scoffed. "He's wearing a baby blue shirt. Straight guys don't wear baby blue shirts."

"I think that's sexist and derogatory."

"And I think you're a pain."

"He could totally be here for me," Harper argued. "He's looking at me just as much as he's looking at you."

"That's because he's trying to ascertain if we're together," Zander volunteered. "He doesn't want to flirt if I have a girlfriend."

"Uh-huh. What about your boyfriend at home?"

"I didn't say I was going to date this guy," Zander pointed out. "I'm merely filming him so I can mess with Shawn. Our relationship is playful."

Harper could think of a few other words to describe it, but there was no point starting a fight in the middle of a busy store. "Can we please finish shopping and get out of here? This place is giving me a headache."

"Sure," Zander replied, shoving his phone into his pocket. "You might want to pick up a pie, though. If you want to make Jared feel safe and loved this evening, comfort food is a must. He loves blueberry pie."

Harper brightened at the suggestion. "Good idea. I should get some whipped cream, too."

"I didn't tell you to turn into a sexual freak while plying him with the pie."

"That's just an added bonus."

THIRTEEN

After three hours of fruitless digging, Jared could no longer bottle up his frustration.

"This is crap!"

Mel, who was focused on Judy Lange's autopsy report, merely arched an eyebrow. "Problem?"

"Yeah, there's a problem. I have a whole bunch of problems."

Mel let loose a sigh that only an older partner could muster. "Lay it on me."

"The hospital Quinn says he turned up in closed three years ago."

Mel stilled. "Closed?"

"Yeah. It was a state hospital in New York. There are news stories all over the place about it closing, something about budget cuts and a psych patient escaping and killing a woman in Central Park. The hospital couldn't recover from the negative press, so the state shut its doors and shuttled the patients to other locations."

"Huh." Mel honestly had no idea what to make of the news. "Quinn was there more than five years ago. It's totally possible that it closed after he left. That happens a lot these days. Hospitals merge or close their doors all the time."

"I know that." Jared tugged on his limited patience. "My problem is that I can't track down this doctor that he mentioned, Irwin Blum. Believe it or not, there are ten people in the city who have that name and I have no idea which one of them is the real deal."

"Maybe you're going about it the wrong way," Mel suggested, choosing his words carefully. He recognized that Jared occasionally turned prickly when his investigative methods were called into question. "Instead of focusing on the names that Quinn supplied, why not pull the names from the old hospital and work your way down from there?"

"Right." Jared brightened. "That's a good idea. I don't know if those people will be harder or easier to track down, but it can't hurt."

"Plus, we need outside verification," Mel reminded him. "Just because Quinn said Irwin Blum was his doctor, that doesn't necessarily make it true."

"You're right." Jared felt like an idiot as he rubbed his forehead. "Why didn't I think of that?"

"Because your mind is full of worry for a certain blonde. Don't take it to heart. Tackle it like you would anything else. One step at a time."

"See, you're not just a crabby old guy who spends his time eating doughnuts," Jared teased. "Zander has you pegged all wrong."

"Zander is going to get a boot in his behind if he's not careful."

"I think he totally deserves it."

HARPER AND ZANDER DECIDED to play holiday angels and deliver a special lunch to Mel and Jared. For her part, Harper wanted to reassure her boyfriend that everything was fine and he had nothing to worry about. For his part, Zander merely wanted to keep Harper's mind on anything other than Quinn. Delivering lunch served a purpose for both of them.

"This is a nice surprise." Jared beamed when he looked up from his computer and saw the takeout bag in Harper's hand. "Are we having lunch?"

"Technically, I already had lunch with Zander." Harper was apologetic as she handed Jared a bag. "The squash soup was so good, though, we thought we would surprise you guys."

"We saw that the cruiser was here — plus both your vehicles — so we decided to be Thanksgiving elves," Zander supplied. "You can thank me this Christmas, Uncle Mel, when it comes time for gifts."

Mel snorted as he accepted the bag his nephew handed him. "Instead, how does being my favorite nephew sound? You can have the title free and clear."

"I'm your only nephew."

"And that's exactly why you're my favorite." Mel winked and shifted his eyes to Harper. "Where have you guys been? Harper looks a little frazzled."

"We were at the grocery store," Zander replied, lowering himself into the chair across from Mel's desk. "Harper doesn't like crowds and she whined like a baby the entire time."

"And, since that's Zander's favorite thing to do, it was something of a territorial dispute," Harper offered. "He's not happy with me usurping his territory."

"I'm not happy with you using the word 'usurp,'" Zander countered, his persnickety personality on full display. "That's a stupid word."

"It seems somehow apt in this particular situation," Jared countered, leaning over so he could give Harper a soft kiss. "You do look a little worn down. Was the store really that busy?"

"You have no idea," Harper replied, squeezing Jared's hand and giving him a warm smile. "If I didn't know better, I would think people got a heads-up about an incoming zombie apocalypse and they're stocking up for the end of the world."

"No zombie apocalypse. We would get a notice on that."

"Good to know." Harper's grin was quick and easy as she sat in the chair across from Jared's desk. "You have no idea how crazy people are acting, though. We actually saw two women fighting over who got the bigger acorn squash. Zander told them it was a myth that bigger is better, but they didn't believe him."

"Ha, ha." Zander rolled his eyes. "I know what you're really saying, and I refuse to fight with you in front of witnesses no matter how low you go."

"Good to know."

"We will fight when it's just the two of us back at the house and I make you start doing food prep, though," he added. "Just wait until I make you shove your hands up that turkey's behind and rip out its guts."

"You always know the sweetest things to say," Harper drawled as Jared rummaged in his takeout bag. "I got your favorite roast beef sandwich and some of the butternut squash soup. It's really good."

"Thank you, Heart. You're such a good provider."

"I do my best." Harper shifted her eyes to Jared's notebook, a series of furious scribbles evident. "Are you having trouble tracking down a suspect in Judy Lange's murder?"

"Oh, well ... ." Jared exchanged a quick look with Mel, uncomfortable.

"We're trying to figure out who Judy had ties with in the area," Mel supplied smoothly. "It's not easy because she moved away years ago and only came back to get money from her mother. The mother is in a home because she has Lupus and doesn't know who Judy was spending her time with."

"You said she was arrested several times when she lived here," Harper noted. "Maybe you should track down the people she was arrested with."

Though agitated he wasn't the one to come up with the avenue of attack, Mel nodded in agreement. "That right there is a good idea, young lady. You think like a police officer. Have you ever considered a career in law enforcement?"

"I don't think most precincts would enjoy my methods," Harper replied dryly. "I mean ... can you imagine the first time I said a ghost told me where to find evidence? I would be locked up."

"Oh, you can be my partner." Jared, his mouth full of roast beef, smiled. "I like your methods."

"Nice." Mel made a face. "If she's your partner, who is my partner?"

Jared inclined his chin toward Zander. "I think you two would be really happy with your partnership."

"Oh, geez. We would kill each other before the end of the first shift."

"That is a blatant lie," Zander countered. "You would thank your lucky stars if you had a partner like me. I'm a great detective."

"What have you ever detected?"

"Today I found a dude in the grocery store and detected he was warm for my form," Zander fired back, not missing a beat as he dug in his pocket. "Harper thought he wanted her, but I think I know better."

"Oh, really?" Mel showed zero interest when Zander showed him the video.

"There was a guy flirting with you in the supermarket?" Jared asked Harper, suddenly alert.

"He didn't even talk to us," Harper countered. "He was simply watching us."

"Me," Zander corrected. "He was watching me because I'm hot and people everywhere want to catch me. Unfortunately for them, I'm already caught. Still, I thought Shawn would like to get a gander at who is out there trying to woo me."

Jared snagged Zander's phone so he could study the video, his eyebrows drawing together after a few seconds of boring video footage. "The guy leaning against the wall?"

Zander nodded. "He wants me."

"Because he's leaning against a wall and staring?"

"You weren't there." Zander made a move to grab his phone back, but Jared kept it out of his reach. "Hey! You can't keep my phone if you're going to make fun of me."

"I had no idea that was the rule, but I'll keep it in mind," Jared said dryly. "I don't suppose you know who this guy is, do you?"

"No." Zander shook his head. "He's simply some random hot guy in the store who wants me."

"He looks familiar." Jared leaned back in his chair as he started the video over from the beginning. "I'm sure I recognize this guy."

Finally showing some interest, Mel swiveled in his chair so he could look at the video. "You're right. I recognize him, too."

"From where?" Harper asked, legitimately curious.

"I don't know." Something niggled at the back of Jared's brain and he jolted forward. "Except I'm almost positive this is one of the people we saw on the video entering the hospital the night Judy Lange was poisoned."

Mel snapped his fingers and nodded. "You're right. He's on that video right before Quinn steps inside. He's one of the faces we couldn't identify, and the lighting was so poor outside we couldn't collect a proper image to run through our search engines."

"We need to run the hospital video again to be sure," Jared said, hitting a few keys before video footage filled his screen. "That was after midnight but before one, right?"

"Yes," Mel confirmed.

Curious, Harper moved so she could stand behind Jared's desk and see the footage for herself. It wasn't that she didn't believe Quinn was at the hospital that night. It was more that she wanted to see his face for herself, perhaps get an inkling of what he was thinking.

Instinctively, Jared slid his arm around her waist as he stood and pointed with his free hand. "Here we go. This is the guy in your video."

Harper leaned forward, not caring in the least that Zander had appeared out of nowhere and was leaning over her back. "That's definitely him. Heck, I think he's wearing the same baby blue shirt as in the video."

"That's what triggered my memory," Jared admitted. "That shirt is not a normal color."

"I told you." Zander was smug as he watched. "There's no doubt that's the same guy."

"I'm going to need you to send me the footage you shot, Zander," Mel instructed, his expression hard to read. "Your image is brighter. We might be able to get a hit in the database if we have a better-quality image."

"Sure." Zander snagged his phone from Jared as Harper rested her hand on top of her boyfriend's wrist to still him from stopping the feed.

"I want to see Quinn," she said quietly.

Jared's gaze was searching. "Why?"

"I don't know." Finding the right words was more difficult than Harper envisioned. "I know you think that Quinn could be a suspect and that's why you don't want him around me."

Even to himself, Jared couldn't admit there was more to his dislike for the man than simply that. "Heart, about this morning ... ."

Harper held up her hand to still him. "No, I'm not angry about this morning. Don't apologize. What happened was a little weird, but I get it. I want to see the footage of him, though."

"I do, too," Zander interjected. "I'm nowhere near as snowed as Harper when it comes to Quinn. That being said, I don't know that I can picture him sneaking into a hospital to kill a woman he barely knew."

"I didn't say I thought he was guilty," Jared hedged, using his mouse to fast forward the footage. "As you can see, though, very few people entered that hospital in the middle of the night. There are only so many people to look at."

Jared had watched the video of Quinn entering the hospital so many times he knew exactly where to stop. "Here we go."

Harper narrowed her eyes as she watched the footage. "It looks like he came from the front parking lot."

"He did."

"If you were going to kill someone, would you park directly in front of the building?"

"The lot was mostly empty," Jared explained. "I don't think most people would worry about being seen."

"If you were coming to commit a murder, though, witnesses would be a worry," Harper persisted. "I'm not standing up for Quinn simply to stand up for him — although I'm certain that's what you believe — but I honestly don't think he's capable of murder.

"He was a decent guy, a nice guy," she continued. "He was a little boring if you believe Zander, but he was a good man."

"He was totally boring ... and kind of bossy," Zander agreed. "He didn't have freaky man nipples and he never wanted to talk with me over coffee. He even put his foot down and said I couldn't have a key to Harper's apartment."

Jared was taken aback. "And you agreed to that, Heart? I couldn't even negotiate a full week without having to share a bed with Zander."

"I didn't agree with it," Harper hedged. "I just kind of let him think I agreed with it."

"That doesn't sound like you."

"I know." Harper was embarrassed. "I was twenty-two. I was young. When he made the request, I was caught off guard and agreed before I realized what I was doing. I was going to talk about it with him again, but the accident happened. It was a long time ago."

Sympathetic to the core, Jared squeezed her hand in a reassuring manner. "Fair enough."

"No matter what you say, I simply can't see Quinn as a murderer," Harper pressed. "He didn't hunt, and he always opened doors for people at restaurants. Killers don't open doors for people."

Jared had to bite back a sigh. "Heart, just because he was polite, that doesn't mean that he's not capable of murder. Still, though, simply turning up at the hospital in the middle of the night doesn't make him guilty. We have no proof he visited Judy Lange's room and poisoned her."

"On top of that, we have no way of knowing if he could get his hands on cyanide," Mel added. "We're in the beginning stages of this investigation, and given Judy Lange's rather colorful history, it's not going to be easy to track down who did this to her."

"What about the other guy, though?" Harper asked. "He could be guilty. I think it's weird that he was at the hospital in the middle of the night, too. Besides that, he's not familiar to me and yet he's been in town for several days."

"Maybe he's not from Whisper Cove," Jared argued. "Maybe he was visiting a relative in the hospital and didn't know about visitation hours." Even to himself, Jared had to admit that sounded lame, but he stuck to his guns. "There are a variety of reasons he might not be the individual we're looking for."

"Except we just saw him at the store a few minutes ago," Harper reminded him. "He's still in town. If he's not from Whisper Cove, why is he hanging out so close to the holidays? Plus — and I didn't want to admit this to Zander because I was certain he would whine if I did — it was creepy the way he stared at us in the store. I was uncomfortable with his attention."

"Then why didn't you call me?" Jared challenged. "If someone was following you around the store and staring, then you should've called me so I could check him out."

"He didn't really follow us," Harper clarified. "He just ... stared."

"At me," Zander added. "He was interested in me, not Harper. I don't think this is your guy. There's no way he could murder a woman and then spend the rest of the week pining for me. That sounds like pure torture."

Even though it was a serious situation, Jared was forced to press his lips together to keep from laughing. "I'm sure it was torture. To see you and not be able to touch you? That's the worst kind of torture."

"I know you're being sarcastic, but that's a true statement." Zander's eyes flashed as he watched the footage of Quinn entering the hospital play for a second time. "I know you probably don't want to hear it, man, but I have to agree with Harper on this one. Quinn is a boring pain in the posterior, but he's never acted in an aggressive fashion as far as I can tell. In fact, he always acts the opposite."

"What do you mean by that?" Jared asked.

"He's passive aggressive. He's kind of a whiner, too. He used to complain about Harper and me going out after dark because it wasn't safe. He was always such a worrywart."

"I'm not a fan of you guys going out late at night either," Jared pointed out. "Do you call me a whiner behind my back, too?"

"I believe I've said it plenty of times to your face," Zander countered. "That doesn't matter, though. I simply don't see Quinn being a killer."

"I hope you guys are right." Jared gave Harper a deliberate squeeze.

"For everyone's sake, I want to follow your instincts on this one. I simply can't discount him at this point. I'm sorry."

"Don't be sorry." Harper's fingers were soft as she combed them through Jared's hair. "Do your job. I'm sure everything will work out how it's supposed to in the end."

"I hope so, too." Jared found he meant it. The pain Harper would go through otherwise was too much to bear. "It's going to be okay either way. Trust me."

FOURTEEN

The search process with the new photo would take time. That meant Jared and Mel needed to fill their afternoon with other avenues of investigation. The first was tracking down a woman named Marley Porter, who just so happened to have an arrest record that overlapped with Judy Lange's several times over.

They found her in a rundown apartment in Sterling Heights, and she wasn't happy to find police officers on the other side of her door when she answered.

"Oh, geez." Marley's hair was straw-like and streaked with gray. She had a cigarette clutched in her hand and wore an unflattering pair of yoga pants. "I didn't do anything. If the landlord is complaining about that chair that went missing when those people were moving, they left it by the dumpster. Everyone knows that you're allowed to take furniture if it's left by the dumpster."

Jared and Mel exchanged a dubious look.

"We're not here about the chair, ma'am," Mel said carefully. "We're here on another matter."

"Well, I didn't steal gas from the BP station last week either. That was a car that looked like mine. I've already explained that."

"We're not with the Sterling Heights Police Department," Jared offered. "We're from Whisper Cove."

The news clearly took Marley by surprise. "Whisper Cove? I haven't been to Whisper Cove in years. Whoever says I did something there ... well ... they're full of it. Why would I possibly go to that raggedy town? There's nothing of interest there."

Jared figured she meant there was nothing worth stealing in Whisper Cove, but he kept the observation to himself. "Ma'am, we're not here to accuse you of anything."

"That's true," Mel confirmed. "We're here to ask questions about a former associate of yours. Judy Lange. We're not interested in how you've been spending your time over the past few years."

"Oh." Puzzlement, deep and fierce, wound its way across Marley's deeply-lined face. "Judy? What has she done?"

"She's dead."

Marley didn't look particularly shocked, but she pushed open her door and ushered the two men inside. "Well, come on. You're letting out all the heat. I don't want to pay for heating the outside."

"Thank you."

Jared did his best not to cringe at the filthy interior of the apartment. It was clear that Marley had been living in the hovel for a number of years. The walls were shiny and coated with a yellow film thanks to the cigarette smoke, and the floor was littered with garbage, including takeout bags and the remnants of forgotten shopping trips. There were so many items on the kitchen table that Jared was torn between the notion that Marley was a serial shoplifter or perhaps a hoarder. Neither option could be ruled out.

"I would offer you something to drink, but I don't want to," Marley said as she settled on the chair in the middle of the living room, leaving the dilapidated couch for Mel and Jared. "What do you want to know about Judy?"

"We understand you were arrested with her twice about fifteen years ago," Mel started.

"I was framed both times," Marley argued. "In fact, I know it's wrong to speak ill of the dead, but Judy was the one who framed me. I should've learned after the first time, but she was apologetic so I let it slide when I shouldn't have. That's on me."

"Yes, well, we don't really want to talk about the logistics of that case other than to understand how Judy operated," Jared supplied. "We're trying to figure out who hated her enough to kill her."

Marley barked out a guttural laugh that was devoid of humor. "Everyone who ever met Judy wanted to kill her."

"Why?" Mel queried. "What can you tell us about her personality?"

"She had a horrible one."

"We would like more information if you have it."

Marley let loose a huge sigh, as if the questions she was being peppered with were so taxing she would soon need a nap. "I don't know what you want me to tell you. Judy was a user. That's not surprising given the crowd we ran with. I haven't seen her in years, though. Like ... a long time. I assumed she had left the area."

"She did," Mel confirmed. "She moved to a variety of different states and had numerous warrants out for her arrest in several states. She returned here at some point, though, and hit her mother up for cash."

"I'm sure her mother didn't jump on that nibble," Marley snorted. "From what I remember, Judy and her mother didn't get along. Judy must've been desperate to come back begging after the way she ran out on her mother without even saying goodbye."

"How do you know she didn't say goodbye?" Jared asked.

"Because the mother came looking for Judy several weeks later and was surprised that her daughter left town without so much as a 'see you, wouldn't want to be you.' She seemed a little sad, but you could tell she was sick, too.

"If you want to know the truth, I think the mother was happy to be rid of her," she continued. "No one wants to admit their kid is a loser and cut ties, but Judy was no prize. It must have been a relief when she ran."

"Was Judy fleeing for a specific purpose?" Mel asked. "I mean ... did she think she would be facing charges anytime soon?"

"That was always the fear in Judy's world. And mine, for that matter. You have to understand, everyone we hung with had some sort of racket going."

"From looking over her record, it seemed Judy was big on investment schemes. How did she pull that off?"

Marley shrugged, seemingly unbothered by the question. "It wasn't hard. She pulled me into a few of those schemes, too. For the record, I did nothing illegal. I made a few calls, did a little research, and I wasn't paid for my time and effort."

"We really aren't here to give you grief," Jared stressed. "Judy Lange was murdered, though, and someone went out of his or her way to make sure she wouldn't have a chance to save herself. If whoever wanted her gone would've waited, there were much less risky avenues that would've been at their disposal."

"I don't think I'm getting the full picture," Marley hedged. "How did she die?"

"Someone poisoned her. In the hospital."

"Oh." Marley made a squinched face. "That seems like a lot of work. As for someone wanting Judy dead, like I told you before, Judy had a lot of enemies. That's what happens when you're in the game. Eventually you screw so many people over that you have no choice but to move on to greener pastures."

"And that's what you think Judy did?"

"I think she was out of ideas for this particular spot of pavement," Marley corrected. "She didn't have the means to run a big scam. That meant she had to stick to smaller scams, like real estate deals."

"And how did those work?"

"Basically we paid a guy to print up fake deeds for us and we sold parcels of land we didn't own to people who thought they would be able to build houses on them," Marley replied. "The key was to find people who were stupid but still had ten grand to pay for the land. They thought they were getting a deal but didn't realize that there was something wrong with the deeds."

Jared was dumbfounded. "But ... what about the title company? What about having a notary around to sign off on documents?"

"That's easier to fake than you realize," Marley answered. "Seriously, though, we only managed to carry off that con a few times. We tried other real estate scams, but they weren't easy and eventually Judy and I parted ways."

"What about the other people you hung with? Did Judy owe any of them money?"

"We all owed each other money. It was not enough to kill over, though. A hundred bucks here or there. Nothing more."

"Some people consider ten dollars worth killing over," Mel noted.

"Not the people I hang with," Marley countered. "We all know we're going to get screwed by each other at some point. That's what you get when you hang around with criminals. It is what it is."

"But ... ."

"No." Marley shook her head, firm. "Listen, I'm not going to pretend to be sorry that Judy's dead. I haven't seen her in a long time and she wasn't a favorite even when we were hanging. I don't know what to tell you. I don't think I have any information you would be interested in."

Jared couldn't help but agree. "Thank you for your time."

AFTER RETURNING TO Whisper Cove, Jared left Mel at the office to check on the search and pointed himself toward the hotel where he knew Quinn was staying.

It was probably a mistake — he told himself that over and over again as he drove — but he had to talk to the man. The more he thought about Quinn's surprise visit so early in the morning, the more his agitation grew.

Quinn was in the downstairs coffee shop flipping through a newspaper when Jared strolled into the lobby. He didn't look surprised to see the police officer, instead exhaling heavily and pointing toward the seat across from him as he folded his newspaper.

"I figured you would stop by."

"Oh, yeah?" Jared smiled as the waitress approached the table. "I'll take a regular coffee, no cream or sweetener. Thank you."

The woman cast him a flirty grin as she turned on her heel and practically bounced to the counter. Her reaction to Jared wasn't lost on Quinn.

"Do you get that a lot?"

"What?"

"Women throwing themselves at you."

Jared cocked his head and held his hands palms out. "I don't really consider that 'throwing herself at me,' but women like to flirt. It comes with the badge."

"How does Harper feel about that?"

The slow fire building in Jared's stomach all day when it came to Quinn's interest in Harper sparked to bonfire size. "Harper and I have a solid relationship. It's built on trust and respect. She knows I would never cheat on her."

"I wasn't suggesting otherwise. It's just ... I've never been one of those guys who walks into a room and finds every set of female eyes on him. That must be entertaining."

"I don't think of myself that way," Jared countered.

"And how do you think of yourself?"

"As a man who wants to balance his personal and professional lives."

Quinn's eyes gleamed with understanding. "Ah. You think I'm getting in the way of that. Come on, you can admit it."

"I think you're starting to make me uncomfortable," Jared said, taking them both by surprise. "I don't know what you're trying to do here, but I feel caught. I love and trust my girlfriend. We're building a life together, and it's not something that's going to fade into the background. Your presence, though, makes me turn bossy and controlling ... and I don't like it."

"I'm not trying to invade your world," Quinn countered. "I know you think that, but I'm not. This isn't easy for me."

"See, the difference between you and me is that I recognize that. I know this isn't easy for you. I get it. Even when I'm angry, I put myself in your position and I can't help but feel a twinge of sympathy, which I don't want to feel because I don't like you."

"Well, at least you can admit it."

"I have no problem admitting it." Jared leaned back in his chair and accepted the coffee the waitress brought without moving his eyes from Quinn's face. He waited until she was gone to continue speaking. "What do you want?"

"What makes you think I want anything?"

"Don't play coy with me," Jared ordered, extending a finger. "What do you want?"

"I don't know." Quinn held his hands out and shrugged, helplessness coursing over his features. "I feel as if I'm caught between two worlds, and I have no idea what I'm supposed to do about that."

"Has it ever occurred to you that you no longer belong in this world?"

"Yes. I'm not trying to force myself on this town, or the people in it. If that's what you're worried about, you can stop. I don't think I belong here."

"Okay, that's a start." Jared licked his lips and debated how to proceed. "What do you want from Harper?"

"I don't want to hurt her."

"You've said that before, and even though I don't like you, I believe it. You want something from her, though. You went out of your way to visit her at work yesterday. You showed up at the house today."

"I don't believe either of those things is illegal."

"No, but they are worrisome," Jared said. "Even if I could get past how weird I find it that you wanted to take my girlfriend for a walk on the beach, why would you possibly want to hang out at GHI for the day?"

Quinn opened his mouth, his eyes furtive, but no sound came out.

"You said you weren't interested in picking up where you left off, but your actions say otherwise," Jared pressed. "That's not fair to Harper. You might not believe this, but I've got her best interests at heart. I don't want her hurt, and I'm afraid the pushing you insist on doing is going to hurt her. Can't you just back off?"

Quinn found his voice. "I don't want to pressure her. That's not my intention. It's just ... I came back to see her. I feel as if I should spend some time with her before ... ."

"Before what?"

"I don't know."

"Before you leave?" Jared prayed he didn't sound too hopeful when he asked the question.

"I already told you I don't intend on staying," Quinn explained. "As for Harper, I don't know what you want me to say. I get she's part of my past, but it feels current to me. It's not about romance, though, no matter what you believe. It's not that."

"I want to help you here, believe you, but I can't help but worry. Harper is the thing I love most in this world, and I feel as if you're putting me in a corner and my only choice is to come out swinging."

"And you don't want that," Quinn surmised. "You don't want to be the guy who attacks the poor soul who lost his memory for five years. You know that will paint you as the villain, and you don't want to be the villain."

"I'm not the villain."

"That's what I said."

"I'm not the villain," Jared repeated. "I want to believe you're not a villain either. No one would blame us for hating one another. This is an awkward position that very few people have ever experienced, and the natural inclination is to embrace the hate. I want to believe I'm more enlightened than that, though."

"But?"

"But I don't know that I am." Jared dug into his pocket and retrieved his phone. "Do you know this man?"

The abrupt change in Jared's demeanor clearly threw Quinn for a loop. "I ... um ... ." He shook his head as he stared at the screen grab the police officer showed him. "Am I supposed to know who that is?"

"I don't know. He was seen entering the hospital the same night as you. We're trying to figure out who he is."

"I'm not local. Wouldn't it be better to ask a local?"

"Harper and Zander don't know who he is."

"Well ... I can't help you." Quinn held up his hands and shrugged. "Is that what you came here to ask me?"

"Amongst other things." Jared downed his coffee in four large gulps and pretended that he wasn't bothered by the taste. "I'm not going to warn you to stay away from Harper. If that's what you're expecting, you're going to have to look elsewhere."

"I hate to break it to you, but Harper is her own person," Quinn pointed out. "She wouldn't like it if you tried to take over her life and warned me away."

"That's the reason I'm not warning you away," Jared admitted. "Everything inside says I should go all alpha and stake my claim on my woman. I'm not going to do that, though."

"I think that's healthy."

"Mostly I'm not going to do that because I don't need to." Jared turned smug. "Zander hates you. He'll put a claim on Harper and you'll be forced to contend with him."

Quinn's lips turned down into a pronounced scowl. "That guy has never liked me. I think he has it in for me."

"He definitely does." Jared tossed a dollar bill on the table to leave as a tip. "I think you want me to draw a line in the sand. That's why you showed up before I left the house this morning. You want Harper and me to fight.

"That's not going to happen," he continued. "I won't let it. Harper is in control of her life. I'm in control of mine. Our lives overlap, and I'm not going to let you screw this up, so whatever you have planned, it's not going to work."

Quinn turned contrite. "I'm not trying to screw up your relationship. She's a touchstone for me, though. She was the most important thing in my life when I left. I can't pretend that's not true now even though it makes you uncomfortable."

"Then don't." Jared was matter-of-fact. "Just remember, things aren't like they were when you left. Relationships change, people move forward and mature. Harper may be your touchstone, but we're together and that's not going to change."

"Fair enough. I respect your relationship boundaries. No matter what you think of me, I'm not the sort of guy to move in on someone else's girl."

"Make sure you don't." With those words, Jared turned on his heel and departed the hotel. He didn't necessarily feel better, but he didn't feel worse either.

That, at least, was something.

FIFTEEN

H arper left Zander to fuss over his gourds at the house. She
wanted some time alone — at least she thought she did — so
the office was out of the question. She considered heading to the
beach. By November's standards, the weather was an unseasonably
warm afternoon (high forties with a lot of sun), so a walk wasn't out
of the question. Since Harper worried she might run into Quinn
there, and that was the last thing she wanted, she did the unthinkable
instead ... and headed to her father's house.

Ever since filing for divorce, Phil Harlow had been going through
a mid-life crisis of sorts. That was what Harper figured anyway. He'd
regressed to the point where he acted as if he was in his twenties.
Actually, since Harper was in her twenties, she offended herself with
the comparison. Phil had been acting much more immature than her.
He simply didn't seem to care what other people thought.

"Hey, Dad."

Harper let herself into her father's rented house without knocking.
He'd recently moved to the place, which was close to the beach, and
spent the bulk of the summer months barbecuing and ogling younger
women in bikinis. Now that the weather had shifted, Phil had moved

the party indoors. While Harper was glad he didn't have women gathering in the living room — that was a real problem when he was holding court close to the water — she wasn't thrilled with her father's television choices.

"What is this?"

Slouched on the couch, a beer on the coffee table in front of him, Phil made a neat picture ... of a man desperately trying to be something he wasn't. "*Southern Charm*. It's about this group of women in the south ... and they're charming."

Harper made a face. "Are you even watching it? If so, you should come up with a better description. That one was ultra-lame."

"I'm not good under pressure." Phil slid his only child a sidelong look. "What's wrong with you?"

"What makes you think something is wrong with me?"

"I can read your moods, kid. You've got an expressive face, and right now that expression seems to be signifying the end of the world. I don't think I can stomach the end of the world before this week's *Real Housewives of Beverly Hills* marathon."

Even though she found her father's antics of late to be irritating, Harper couldn't hold back her smirk. "You just like saying things to throw people off, don't you?"

"I have no idea what you're talking about."

"Yeah, yeah." Harper rolled her neck and relaxed on the couch, her eyes drifting toward the television screen. "Did you hear my ex-boyfriend came back from the dead?"

As far as opening lines went, it wasn't Harper's finest offering. She had no idea how to broach the subject, though, so she went straight for the jugular.

Phil almost choked on his beer he was so surprised by the comment. "Excuse me?"

"Quinn is back." When Phil didn't immediately say anything, she barreled forward. "Quinn Jackson, that guy I dated until he was in the car accident and wandered away from the scene, the one everyone thought died in the woods ... um ... he's back from the dead."

"I remember Quinn." No longer interested in his program, Phil hit the remote-control button and switched off the television. "Are you saying he's alive?"

"He showed up a few days ago. He had amnesia after the accident. He moved to New York." Even as the words slipped out of her mouth, Harper realized how ridiculous they sounded. "He had a head injury and only started remembering things a few weeks ago. He came back to see me and clear things up with the cops."

Phil was utterly flabbergasted. "How come I'm just hearing about this?"

Harper held her hands out and shrugged. "I thought everyone in town knew."

"You should have called."

"So you could do what?"

"I don't know." Phil's frustration bubbled over. "I'm still your father. I know you don't see it that way lately, but as your parent, I demand to know certain things about your life. Your dead boyfriend showing up would be one of those things."

Despite herself, Harper was amused. "Of course I still see you as my father. Why wouldn't I?"

"Because, the last little bit hasn't been a shining example of what I'm capable of," he admitted, sheepish. "Your mother drives me crazy, though. I can't help it. I *have* to fight with her. I don't want to draw you into the fights, so I don't visit as much as I should. That's on me."

"Dad, you don't have to worry about that." Harper awkwardly patted her father's knee. As much as she didn't want to admit it, she'd found some of the fights her parents engaged in rather amusing. Of course, she also found them tedious. "You know I'm always on your side no matter what, and that's only partially because I like watching Mom melt down."

"I know." Phil poked her side and offered a wan smile. "I still love you, Harper. This is big news. I mean ... huge news. How are you dealing with this?"

"I don't know."

"You don't know?"

"It's a mess, Dad." Harper's eyes turned glassy. "When I first saw him, I thought for sure I was dreaming. I've dreamed of him coming back before, like it was some big mistake and he wasn't really dead or missing ... just delayed."

"I think that's probably normal."

"Is it?" Harper cocked an eyebrow. "Zander and I were out at Betty Miller's field because she claims her scarecrow is coming to life and haunting the property — I really need to follow up on that tomorrow because I've been distracted — and when we went back to Zander's vehicle after running some tests, he was waiting next to the truck."

"How does he look? I mean ... is he deformed from the accident or anything? What? If this were a movie, he would be deformed."

"You watch way too much television, Dad."

"It's a legitimate question."

"He looks largely the same, although different," Harper supplied. "His hair is a little lighter and he has a beard. His eyes are the same, though."

"What about his personality? You said he had amnesia. Does he act the same?"

"Kind of."

Phil stared hard into his daughter's eyes. "Do you want to expand on that?"

"I don't know what to say." Harper felt helpless as she slouched lower on the couch. "I know this is going to sound terrible, but I'm starting to wonder if I ever knew him at all. I haven't spent a lot of time with him — a few hours here and there — and he hung out at GHI yesterday.

"He seems gregarious and engaged in conversation, and he asks the appropriate questions about my life," she continued. "There's no connection between us, though. Quinn came back because he felt he owed me an explanation, but the thread that should be tying us together is absent."

"Harper, you were young when you dated Quinn."

"I know."

"You were barely out of college. You and Zander were running around doing your ghost thing, but back then you were aimless and without focus. Of course you didn't have a deep connection with Quinn. You were too young to maintain it."

"I had a deep connection with Zander," Harper argued. "We formed an even deeper connection when we were kids."

"That's different. He's your best friend. He's been around through thick and thin. Quinn was never around for anything more than a few drunken parties. And, if you want me to be totally honest, I never really liked him."

The admission hit Harper hard and fast. "You watched football and stuff with him."

"I *pretended* to like him," Phil clarified. "I did that for you. I mean ... I didn't hate him. He was too bland to hate. I certainly didn't love him, though. I thought you could do better."

"But ... ." Harper had no idea what to make of her father's words.

"Harper, you were barely an adult back then and your mother and I were doing our best to hold onto the last shreds of our marriage, even though we didn't want you to know that," Phil explained. "We didn't want to add to what you were dealing with at the time by telling you we thought your boyfriend was a bit of a tool."

Harper's mouth dropped open. "Mom didn't like him either?"

"Again, it's not that we hated him. It's just ... he was annoying. He was always sucking up. There was nothing genuine about him. He pretended to be interested in what I had to say, but I could tell it was all for show."

"Why didn't you say something?" Harper felt like a teenager all over again. "If you'd said something, maybe ... ." She trailed off, uncertain.

"Maybe what?" Phil pressed. "Maybe you would've broken up with him and he never would've gotten into the accident and been left with amnesia? Maybe then you wouldn't have blamed yourself and felt guilty for years? Don't you think I've considered that myself?"

"It's not that I felt guilty," Harper hedged. "It's that ... okay, I felt guilty. He was only here for me, though. He stayed in the area because of me."

"That's not on you, kid." Phil was firm. "You were young. Most people kiss a lot of frogs before they find the prince. I just figured Quinn was one of those frogs. You would date him for a bit and then figure out you didn't belong with him.

"Unfortunately for you, that never happened," he continued. "Once he died — or everybody thought he died — you stagnated for a bit. You blamed yourself. No one could talk you down from what you were feeling. Zander was so worried he insisted the two of you live together because he wanted to keep an eye on you."

"He phrased it a different way when he suggested it to me," Harper grumbled, annoyance threatening to take over. "He said it would be a smart financial decision."

"The fact that you fell for that shows how out of sorts you were at the time." Phil's grin was rueful. "Harper, don't dwell on it. You came out the other side. You and Zander have built a strong business. You know who you are and aren't afraid to live the life you want to live."

"All of that is well and good," Harper hedged. "I guess I can deal with most of that ... although I'm not happy to know you thought I was dating a putz."

"I don't believe I used that word, but it's not incorrect."

"Ha, ha." Harper rolled her neck and stared at the ceiling. "Believe it or not, Quinn is not my big concern right now. It's Jared. He seems ... odd."

Instead of clucking with sympathy, Phil barked out a raucous laugh. "Odd? You think he's acting odd? Oh, why ever would that be?"

"Nobody needs your sarcasm," Harper grumbled, folding her arms over her chest. "I came here for the male perspective. I didn't come here to be laughed at."

"Well, you're going to have to put up with both." Phil turned serious. "Are you honestly surprised that Jared isn't okay with Quinn's miraculous resurrection?"

"I would think he'd be happy. Quinn isn't dead. That's a good thing."

"I doubt very much that Jared wants Quinn dead," Phil noted. "It would be easier if his feelings were that cut and dry. Jared isn't upset because Quinn is alive. He's upset because he has a rival for your heart."

"He doesn't, though. I love Jared. I don't love Quinn."

"I know. You never loved Quinn."

"Everyone keeps saying that to me," Harper groused. "I know it myself, but people keep dropping that bomb as if they're trying to enlighten me. It's ridiculously annoying."

"People are simply trying to help."

"It doesn't feel helpful."

"That's because you're in a gloomy place." Phil sipped his beer before offering it to Harper. "Do you want to take the edge off?"

Harper shook her head. "If I start drinking now, I may never stop."

"Oh, stop being dramatic." Phil was obviously enjoying himself, a fact that set Harper's teeth on edge. "As for Jared, as much as he knows that you love him, it has to be difficult to see the man who changed the course of your life back in town and sniffing around. That can't possibly be a comfortable scenario."

"Quinn didn't change the course of my life," Harper scoffed.

"Honey, his death did." Phil gentled his voice. "Had you been allowed to end the relationship on your terms, Quinn would be no more than the guy you trot out funny stories about when you're drunk and reminiscing. The fact that he died — or you thought he died — froze you in place for a bit.

"It wasn't that you loved him so much that you were crushed into oblivion, it was that you got weighed down by guilt and didn't allow yourself to let go of his memory," he continued. "Personally, I'm glad Quinn came back to tell you what happened. Now you can let him go."

"That's the problem, though, I don't think I'm the one hanging onto him. I think Quinn is hanging onto me."

"Well, I'm not an expert, but that might be normal," Phil offered. "If he's only recently started remembering things, you might be an anchor to the past he needs to rediscover. Once his emotions settle, he'll realize what everyone in town does."

"That we were never right for each other?"

"That, and the fact that you and Jared are meant for each other. It can't be easy on the guy. Even though I'm sure he didn't want you to suffer, part of him had to be annoyed that you weren't sitting around pining for him.

"You moved on, though," he continued. "You fell in love with a great guy, made plans to move in together, and basically eradicated most of the memories of Quinn from your life."

Harper rubbed her cheek as she regarded her father with plaintive eyes. "So ... what do you think I should do to make Jared feel more secure and get Quinn out of town?"

Phil's answer was simple. "Just love Jared the way you always do. The rest of it will shake out how it's supposed to. There's a bigger power at play here, and things always turn out how they're supposed to. Trust me."

HARPER PARKED AT THE new house rather than heading to the current one. She was anxious to head inside, maybe find a project to busy herself with. She needed a distraction, and mindless housework seemed like a good way to start.

She had her keys out, but they were unnecessary. The front door was open. When she pushed open the door and heard The Rolling Stones playing in the next room, she couldn't stop herself from smiling. Jared loved The Rolling Stones, and he was clearly here to do some thinking, too.

She quietly placed her keys on the table by the door before moving through the house, her eyes lighting when she realized Jared was cleaning cupboards while singing softly to himself. He looked serious, intent on his task, but there was also something adorable about the way he swung his hips as he scrubbed.

"All you're missing is a maid's uniform," Harper teased, causing Jared to swivel quickly. "Oh, I'm sorry. I didn't mean to frighten you."

"You scared the crap out of me," Jared admitted, his expression rueful. "I didn't know you were here. I didn't hear the front door open."

"I think that's because you're rocking out to the oldies."

"Yeah, well ... ." Jared licked his lips as he watched Harper shed her heavy coat. "Where have you been? I thought you would be with Zander at the house, but he was knee deep in cooking preparations and said you'd been gone for a good two hours."

Harper recognized what he wasn't saying. He wanted to know if she'd been hanging out with Quinn. "I was with my father," she volunteered. "We had a long conversation about life, ex-boyfriends coming back from the dead, and some weird show about Southern belles."

"Oh." The relief emanating from Jared was palpable. "Well, that's good."

"It is," Harper agreed, her heart going gooey when she realized that Jared was trying so hard to do right by her that he was ignoring his own needs. "Hey, Jared?"

"What?"

"I love you."

Jared's eyes were serious when they locked with hers. "I know. I love you, too."

"No, I don't think you do. I mean ... *know*. I get that you love me. You're worried about Quinn, though, and I really wish you wouldn't."

"I'm not worried about Quinn." Jared said the words with bravado, but worry remained firmly rooted in his eyes. "I'm fine. You don't have to worry about me, just like I'm not worried about Quinn."

"Uh-huh." Harper wasn't convinced. Also, she was no longer willing to tie herself into knots of fear. "Let's not worry, shall we?" She strode across the room and wrapped her arms around Jared, grabbing a fistful of his hair and giggling when he widened his eyes. "Let's focus on each other and leave all the worry outside."

Jared hugged Harper against him. "I think that sounds like a fabulous idea."

"We can even get pizza delivered ... once we've spent a little quality time together, of course."

"That sounds like a plan." Jared lowered his lips until they were a hair's breath away from Harper's mouth. "Do you want to focus on me first, or shall I focus on you?"

"We'll do it together. That's the way we work best."

"It really is."

SIXTEEN

A makeshift picnic on the living room floor was just what the relationship doctor ordered. They spread out on a blanket, made plans for the future, and laughed about Zander's upcoming Thanksgiving nightmare.

"I know he likes to fuss about things, but I don't think I've seen him this excitable over a meal before," Jared noted as he wiped his hands and closed the pizza box. "How come he's so worked up?"

"Because, in his head, he's billing this as our last holiday together," Harper replied, her hair mussed from rolling around on the floor for an hour before they placed their dinner order. "He can't help himself."

"That's ridiculous. We're still sharing holidays. You're going to be across the road, not in another state."

"He can't see that far into the future. It will be okay. He can't help himself from getting worked up. It's part of his personality."

"Well, I wish he would knock it off." Jared idly took Harper's hand and flipped it over so he could trace the lines on her palm. "You seem to be in a better mood than earlier."

"I wasn't in a bad mood earlier."

"You weren't in a good mood."

"I guess not." She pursed her lips. "I went to see my father because I wanted to talk about men, you in particular. I've been struggling with how to make you feel secure given what's going on."

"Don't worry about me."

"I believe you're the one who told me that worry comes with the job when you're in a healthy relationship," she pointed out. "Do you know what my father did when I told him what was going on? By the way, he hadn't heard about Quinn's return. I think that proves he's watching a bit too much Bravo."

"What did he say? Did he tell you to kiss my boo-boo and mend my broken heart?" Jared's eyes gleamed with mirth.

"He laughed at me."

"What do you mean?"

"He laughed at me, at both of us, at all of us."

Jared bristled. "I don't particularly think any of this is funny."

"That's the point. I said I was worried because you were acting out of sorts, and he thought I was the funniest person ever. He said of course you were acting out of sorts, my ex-boyfriend came back from the dead and anyone who acted normally under those circumstances would be the individual to worry over."

"Did you tell him the part where your ex-boyfriend might be involved in a murder?"

Sheepish, Harper lowered her eyes. "No, I left that part out. I didn't want to get into a huge discussion with him, especially since I don't feel I know all the facts."

Jared shifted, alert. "I'm not keeping anything from you."

"That's not what I meant. I don't think I understand everything. I want you to lay it out for me so we can talk about things together. I feel as if I've been a bit out of it when it comes this case, and I want to know what you know."

"Okay." Jared leaned so his back was pressed against the wall. "Where do you want me to start?"

"With Vicky Thompson. I don't feel as if I know enough about her."

"Well, her real name is Judy Lange."

"I know that much."

"She was a grifter, running a series of cons." Jared launched into his story. "The local ones were mostly real estate scams. Anyone with any knowledge of how a real estate transaction works would've run the other way, but they were smart. They put together a series of deals that were too good to be true and then tailored them toward people who had money to spend, but not enough money to get the real thing."

"Ah." Harper bobbed her head knowingly. "I get what you're saying. Like ... you can't have this great house, but how would you like a piece of land that will double in worth in a few years? Something like that, right?"

"Exactly. I like how smart you are." Jared tweaked her nose. "One of the business deals gone sour was for a piece of property on M-59. Obviously that looked like a good deal because that stretch of road went from dirt to a business extravaganza in under two decades. The piece of empty land has been left that way because it's swampland, though, which none of these brainiacs handing over their money bothered to check."

"So, basically we're talking ten grand, or even five grand a pop, right?"

"Exactly. Judy and her friends — the one we met, Marley, was a true joy — took the money in each case and ran. Eventually, Judy got to the point where she had no more takers on her con so she started moving between states."

"You said she had warrants out for her arrest in other states," Harper noted. "Did she ever do time?"

"No, she seemed to have impeccable timing. She managed to skip town at exactly the right moment and managed to evade arrest in most circumstances. The two times she was arrested she posted bail and then never showed up for subsequent court appearances."

"She was sneaky."

"She was."

"So, why come back here?" Harper queried. "I know you said

something about her trying to get money from her mother, but how long would that money really have lasted? I don't get why she came back."

"I don't understand why she came back either," Jared admitted. "She had to know her mother wasn't going to finance her. I mean ... I guess she could've been desperate, but Judy Lange sounds like the sort of woman who managed to survive no matter what."

"She was going under another name, though," Harper pointed out. "She was clearly worried about people finding out she was back in town."

"I'm not sure if she was worried about the police looking for people she wronged in the past. Either way, it was probably smart for her to operate under a fake name. That way she could keep both factions off her."

"You saw her, though. She was in an accident. How did she seem?"

"Shaken up," Jared admitted, searching his memory for fragments of the time he spent with the woman. "She was a good actress. I never thought, not even for a second, that she was pretending to be someone else. To us, it simply seemed as if she'd gotten into an accident and needed to go to the hospital. It would've required some paperwork and nothing else."

"Did Mel feel the same way?"

"Are you insinuating Mel is a better detective than me?"

"Of course not. It's just ... he knows that stretch of road. I thought maybe he might notice if there was something odd about the way things played out."

Jared turned thoughtful. "Huh. I didn't even consider that." He rolled his neck until it cracked. "You know, that's a very interesting theory, Heart. The accident wasn't fatal, though, so we decided against calling the state police accident reenactment team. We took some photographs but that's it. I don't know that we can go back and look at the facts of the accident and come up with a different answer."

"If there were no other vehicles around, then it would make sense not to spend a lot of time on the accident scene."

"I think you're making excuses to cover my laziness because you're soft on me."

Harper kissed the corner of his mouth. "I won't let anyone talk badly about you ... including you."

"Good to know." Momentarily overcome by love, Jared cupped the back of her head. "I feel the same way about you."

"We're mushy tonight, huh?"

"Very."

"I still want to hear the rest of the information."

"Right." Jared released her head and straightened. "Mel said that the scene reminded him of Quinn's accident. That made me uncomfortable because ... well ... I'm always uncomfortable talking about guys you used to date. Why do you think I hate Jason Thurman?"

Harper snickered at the mention of a friend she dated very briefly in high school, one who recently returned to open a restaurant. "You and Jason don't hate each other. You enjoy busting each other's balls."

"There are times I hate him."

"You do not. You just want people to think you hate him. I know better. You're a big marshmallow."

"Only where you're concerned." Jared tickled her ribs and caused her to squeal.

"Not yet! Not yet!" She slapped at his hands. "We can't do that again until I hear the rest."

"Fine." Jared wasn't thrilled with the delay, but he was a patient man. "She seemed fine, if a bit shaky. That's normal when it comes to a rollover accident. She was transferred to the hospital because of her head injury even though she said she was fine."

"Do you think she said she was fine because she wanted to escape?"

"In hindsight, that's exactly what I think. However, I didn't recognize that at the time. She was transported to the hospital and kept for observation."

"Then she died out of the blue."

"And Quinn and that other guy — whom we have yet to find an

identity on, in case you're wondering — both entered the facility not long before the poison was delivered."

Harper rubbed her hands against her bare knees as she got comfortable. "I know you think I'm sticking up for Quinn because ... well, because I'm a naive little girl or something ... but how could he have possibly gotten his hands on cyanide when he just got back to town?"

"He could've brought it with him."

"But ... why? What would be the point? How could he possibly know that he would bear witness to an accident almost exactly like the one he went through? Why kill Judy after witnessing that accident? Do you think the mere sight of it was enough to turn him into a homicidal maniac?"

Jared hated to admit it, but she had a point. "I don't know. That's the part that makes all of this so very uncomfortable. I can't find a motive."

"So ... he's obviously not guilty."

"I don't want to start a fight — no, really, I don't — but are you sure you don't simply believe that because it's easier than facing the alternative?"

"I guess that's possible, but I don't think it's likely," Harper countered. "Still, I will give you that it's a little too coincidental to be comfortable that Quinn just happened to be at the scene of a similar accident. What are the odds of that?"

"Not good. We clearly don't have evidence on him, though. I'm still trying to track down if his amnesia story is real and not having a lot of luck."

Harper froze, Jared's words causing her head to spin. "What?"

Jared realized his mistake too late. "Oh, um ... ."

"You're checking into his amnesia story?" Harper was dumbfounded. "You don't believe he's telling the truth, do you?"

"I don't know." Jared chose his words carefully. "I don't want you to get upset about this. We have no proof of anything."

"I'm not upset." In truth, Harper found she wasn't upset ... or even hurt. She was, however, curious. "I need more information, though. Why are you checking on his story?"

"Because he's a suspect in a murder investigation," Jared answered honestly.

"So ... are you saying you wouldn't have checked out his story if he didn't happen to be present at the accident scene? If he didn't visit the hospital at an odd time, would you have let it go?"

Jared's first instinct was to say "yes." Upon further reflection, however, he shook his head. "I would've checked up on his story regardless. I would like to pretend I'm this great guy who would simply react on faith, but that's not me. I would've checked."

Harper's lips curved. "I'm glad you can admit it. I'm also glad you're checking."

"You are?" Jared couldn't conceal his surprise. "I thought you would be angry when you found out."

"I'm not happy that it's necessary," she clarified. "I understand the need to check, though. His story covers everything but, the more I think about it, the more bothered I am by the simple fact that nobody in New York bothered to call other states to check on missing-person reports."

"Yes, well, that bothers me, too," Jared admitted, running his hand over the back of his short-cropped hair. "Here's the thing: The hospital Quinn claims to have stayed at over the first several months of his recovery is gone."

"Gone? Like ... it's not there?"

"Like it closed," Jared corrected. "Three years ago."

"Well, that's possible." Harper tilted her head to the side, considering. "It sounds a little convenient, doesn't it?"

"Very convenient. The chief of staff at the hospital was listed in some news stories, so I've been trying to track him down. I have a call out, but he hasn't returned it yet. I've also tried calling the board of directors, but none of them recognize Quinn's photograph or story."

"I hate to beat a dead horse, but that's entirely possible," Harper noted. "The board of directors wouldn't be familiar with the patients at the hospital. They're more of an oversight committee.

They have very little to do with the day-to-day operations of the facility."

"I get that. That's why I'm waiting for the chief of staff."

"What about the doctor Quinn supplied?" Harper asked the obvious question. "Have you called him?"

"He supplied two doctors, a man and a woman. One is his therapist. I've only managed to get one of them on the phone."

"Which one?"

"The female." Now it was Jared's turn to squirm as discomfort rolled over him. "Her name is Lydia Hitchman. I called her, and she answered right away. She confirmed Quinn's story."

"Well, that's something, right?"

"Except the number he supplied was a cell and she was at home. I have no way of confirming she worked at the closed hospital until I talk to the chief of staff. And, oh, she and Quinn are involved."

Jared hadn't meant to blurt out the information in that manner. He meant to be more sympathetic, or at least comforting. The surprised look on Harper's face reminded him of that.

"I didn't mean ... ."

Harper held up her hand to silence him. "It's okay."

"No, it's not okay. I should've phrased that a different way, or braced you for it or something."

Instead of being angry, though, Harper barked out a laugh. "Did you really think I would be upset?"

"Maybe."

"I'm not upset." Harper waved off Jared's apology. "We weren't together. It's not as if he cheated on me. For the record, if you were the one who had a secret doctor girlfriend, I would be broken-hearted."

"No stupid doctor could take your place in my heart."

"Good to know." Harper leaned closer so Jared could rest his hand on her knee. "No one could replace you in my heart either. That's not what this is about, though. It's about Quinn."

"It is, and I can't take some random woman's word over the phone that the story Quinn told is real. I need more confirmation than that."

"I don't blame you." That was the truth. Harper understood exactly where Jared was coming from. "You need outside confirmation. I have a question, though, and I want an honest answer."

"Do you think I would lie to you? After everything we've come to mean to each other, after everything we've gone through, do you honestly think I would lie?"

"No," Harper responded without hesitation. "I do think you would slide around things if you thought you were protecting me, though. I don't want you to do that. I want a straight answer."

"Okay. Shoot."

"If you find out Quinn has been lying from the start, that none of the things he said are true, what will that prove? I mean ... what will you do?"

"I honestly don't know." Jared had thought about the question so many times he figured he should have an answer by now. He simply didn't. "We'll probably have to start an investigation. A lot of money was spent on the search for Quinn. You can leave a life without breaking the law, give no forwarding address, and start over. You cannot leave a mess the way Quinn did and not answer some questions."

"That makes sense." Harper was thoughtful. "What other reason could he have for leaving besides what he said?"

"I don't know, Heart. I've never looked into his past. I've thought about it because I was curious, but ultimately I didn't because it didn't seem fair to you."

"Maybe you should look into his past."

Surprise washed over Jared, a strong wave of relief along for the ride. "Do you want me to? I can do that, maybe find out exactly what he was doing before he disappeared. I'm sure Mel has at least started a cursory search. I can build on it."

"I wouldn't mind knowing," Harper admitted. "I want to believe the amnesia story. It makes me feel better. If it's not true, though, we should probably get ahead of this problem. It's better to do it now than wait for trouble to track us down."

"You're very wise."

"I am."

"You're really pretty, too."

Harper's cheeks heated as Jared reached for her waist. "I take it that means the talking portion of our evening is done."

"Definitely. You're on the dessert menu, and I'm ready for my treat."

SEVENTEEN

Jared and Harper were in a much better place when they returned to the other house and retired for the evening. Zander and Shawn were already in bed, so it was impossible to catch up on all the gossip until the following morning over breakfast.

"Your father is watching *Southern Charm?*" Zander was baffled and delighted. "I knew we were television soul mates. I'm totally going over there to watch new episodes with him from now on since you guys make fun of me when I try to watch it here."

"I don't think we make fun of you," Shawn countered, sipping his juice. "I think we simply vote against you when it comes time for group viewing."

"That was a lovely way to put it," Zander drawled. "I know when I'm being persecuted, though."

"Poor Zander." Jared was in high spirits as he ate his toast. "We'll try to take your feelings into consideration from here on out. We'll make you the center of our world."

"That's all I ask."

Harper's smile was so wide it almost swallowed her entire face. "Speaking of that, Zander, I need to run back out to Betty's house and look at the scarecrow again."

Whatever happiness Zander was feeling evaporated. "That scarecrow is not possessed."

"I happen to agree. We were hired for a job, though. I need to check the scene again to make sure that nothing odd is going on out there. Tomorrow is Thanksgiving, and I don't want to do it then."

"I can't go with you. I have a bunch of stuff to do around here, including deviled eggs and my famous stuffing marinade. Put it off until the day after Thanksgiving."

The suggestion didn't sit well with Harper. "I was thinking that today would be better. I don't want to leave her hanging."

"I hate to agree with Zander — on pretty much anything — but I'm not sure I want you walking around out there on your own," Jared interjected. "Quinn found you there before. He might check again. I don't want you alone with him until I have more information."

"Quinn would never hurt me."

"Probably, but he is a suspect in a murder. Can't you hold off? I have an extended weekend. I planned to do a bunch of things around the new house, but I can take some time to visit the field with you Friday. Wait until then."

"I would rather get it out of the way now," Harper persisted. "I don't want to leave Betty in the lurch. She's a nice, if somewhat tempestuous, woman who has a potentially hazardous problem."

"The scarecrow is not possessed," Zander persisted. "There is no problem ... other than she's crazy."

"Yes, well ... ." Harper trailed off, something occurring to her. "What if I take Molly with me? She's always complaining we don't have her in the field enough. This is a literal field, and it will be perfectly safe. I doubt Quinn will bother tracking me down out there, but if he does, I won't be alone."

"I guess I can live with that," Jared muttered. "I would appreciate it if you texted me when you arrived and left, though. That way I won't worry."

"I think you'll worry anyway," Harper teased, leaning closer in an enticing manner. "That's because I'm your favorite person in the world and you can't stop yourself from thinking about me twenty-four hours a day."

"You're not wrong." Jared planted a firm kiss on her mouth. "I'll probably be in the office making calls and tracking things down for the bulk of the day. I might leave for a bit, but I doubt it will be for long. Once we're both done with our work today, I want to put all of this behind us for a bit. Do you think you can handle that?"

"Yes. I would love to spend the weekend handling you." Harper was as giddy as Jared, and their overt flirting was enough to make Zander roll his eyes.

"Ugh. You guys are so gross sometimes. Honestly, I'm glad you're moving out and abandoning me. That way I won't have to watch you do *this* any longer."

"We're doing it to make you happy," Jared supplied. "You're the center of our world, after all. We live to serve you."

Instead of playing into the sarcasm, Zander merely smiled. "Keep it up. You're doing a good job."

COMPUTER WORK WAS JARED'S least favorite part of the job. He wasn't a fan of sitting behind a desk and pecking away at a keyboard. Unfortunately for him, that's all he could accomplish the day before Thanksgiving.

"You must have run a background check on Quinn Jackson when he disappeared," Jared noted as he swiveled to face his partner, who was busy working on his computer. "What did you come up with?"

Mel, a pumpkin spiced latte in his hand, didn't appear surprised by the question. "Of course I ran a background search. It's standard protocol in situations like what occurred with him."

"Did you find anything?"

"Yes."

That wasn't the answer Jared was expecting. "What did you find?"

"I found a whole lot of things, but none of it seemed to matter given what went down. I mean ... he was in an accident. That's not in dispute. A great deal of blood was found at the scene, which seemed to indicate that he was injured gravely in the rollover and it wasn't anything from his past that came back to haunt him."

Jared was officially intrigued. "You must have found something good. Otherwise you wouldn't be playing coy like this."

"I don't know how good it is," Mel cautioned. "I did find a few things that gave me pause, though. You have to understand, at the time I didn't think it was smart to tell Harper what I uncovered because she was grieving. Zander was worried enough about her becoming obsessed with searching the woods that he insisted they move in together. I didn't want to add to things."

"Well, she's fine now ... and I want to know. I'm going to dig deep myself, but if you already have the information, you'll save me some time."

"I have the information." Mel opened the bottom drawer of his desk and came back with a blue file folder. He handed it to Jared and waited until his partner opened it to continue. "In a nutshell, Quinn Jackson was not a good student. He also, apparently, wasn't a very good man."

Jared's stomach twisted at Mel's choice of phrasing. "Meaning?"

"He went to Northwood University. It's a business school in Midland. He met Harper and Zander when they were all in college. Their campuses were about thirty minutes apart, and Harper met Quinn at a bar one night. They didn't immediately start dating, instead striking up a flirty friendship, but when they did get involved it was initially casual.

"The thing about Northwood is that there's a different atmosphere there," he continued. "The students are more serious — not to say there aren't serious students at Central Michigan University, but they enjoy a good party there, too — and the degrees are more stylized, if you will, at Northwood."

"Basically you're saying that the students who attend come out with a grand plan," Jared surmised. "They're all focused on high-paying jobs and very few of them are looking to take a year off and find themselves."

"You're very good at this." Mel winked. "I pulled Quinn's transcript from the school. I'm still not sure why I did it. I guess I was curious. There was a notation about some disciplinary action while he was there, and I called to get more information.

"I had to jump through hoops because of privacy laws, but I convinced the dean that it was important because Quinn was in imminent danger," he continued. "The dean informed me that Quinn had quite the reputation ... as a ladies' man who liked to steal from his girlfriends."

Jared's mouth dropped open. "And you didn't think this was important to mention?"

"I don't know that it ties into Quinn's disappearance," Mel shot back. "How could the fact that he seduced one of his female professors and convinced her to pay for an apartment and a car lease play into his death two years later?"

"It's a pattern of behavior," Jared shot back. "Harper had a right to know about this."

"I made a judgment call," Mel argued. "It might not have been the right call at the time, but I was convinced Quinn was dead. I didn't see the point of tainting her memories after the fact. I couldn't see how it would make things better, and I believed there was a very real chance it would make matters worse."

Even though he annoyed, Jared understood his partner's protective instincts. "Okay. I get it. After he showed back up, though, why didn't you say something then?"

"I couldn't remember all the details. I stuffed the file in a cabinet at home and forgot about it ... until I went looking last night. When I was going through the files I managed to reacquaint myself with some of the facts and, sad as I am to admit it, there's some pertinent information in there."

Jared was practically salivating. "Show me."

"I figured you would say that."

"SO, BETTY THINKS THIS thing is possessed?"

Molly wasn't nearly as thrilled to be pulled into the field as Harper envisioned. That probably had something to do with the fact that she was cuddled up with Eric on the couch in the GHI office when Harper called. Since things had been slow — the after-Halloween lull always worked that way — she knew declining the invitation was a bad idea.

"She does," Harper confirmed, flipping the switch on an EMF reader as she slowly paced around the scarecrow. "She swears up and down she's seen it moving out here, although this is my second visit and it's done nothing but sit there the entire time."

"This thing isn't real." Molly poked her finger into the scarecrow's mask hole and made a disgusted face. "Ugh. It's all wet and gross in here."

"That's because it's stuffed with straw," Harper pointed out, her attention firmly on the device in her hand. "It's also a rainy time of year. Of course it's gross and wet in there."

Molly's tone was accusatory. "You could've warned me."

"I thought it was common sense."

"Well, apparently I'm devoid of common sense." Molly pulled away from the scarecrow and started circling the figure. "That's what Eric says, by the way. He says that I skipped the line the day they were handing out common sense."

Harper smirked at the young woman's forlorn expression. "Molly, I hate to break it to you, but that's an old saying. My father used to say the same thing about me when I was a teenager. It's fine. You'll outgrow it."

"That's easy for you to say," Molly complained. "Everyone you come into contact with thinks you're a genius. Eric says he adores me, but I'm a pain in the butt and I need to think before I do things. Do you know how annoying that is to hear?"

"As a matter of fact, I do. Jared says the same thing to me at least once a month."

Molly brightened considerably. "He does? You mean ... it's not just me?"

"Of course it's not just you." Harper didn't fancy herself an expert on men — especially in light of recent developments — but she opted to impart whatever wisdom she had to offer on Molly all the same.

"All men think they're smarter than women. Even when a man acknowledges you're smart, he still needs to feel as if he's smarter."

A cracking sound filled the air as Molly snapped her gum. She didn't seem thrilled to hear Harper's take on the nature of men. "Doesn't that drive you crazy?"

"Only a little."

"It drives me a lot crazy."

"Yes, well, get used to it. It's not going to change."

"It's important to be the change you want to see in the world," Molly countered. "I read that somewhere, although I forget where. That's how I want to be, though. I want to change the world ... and if I have to convince Eric I'm smart to do it, I'll simply hold him down until he agrees I'm brilliant."

Harper's grin was easy and wide. "That sounds like a great idea. I bet that works out exactly how you envision it."

"I bet it will, too."

"Men don't equate wrestling with sex or anything. All that grappling won't end with you two in bed and him congratulating himself for being the smartest man in the world. That would never happen."

Molly's smile faltered. "Huh. I didn't even think of that."

"Yes, well, you haven't been at this as long as me."

"I guess not." Her expression thoughtful, Molly scuffed her shoes against the ground and internally debated how to broach a new topic. Finally, she simply decided to go for it. "How are things with Quinn? By the way, I think he's really nice. Do you think you'll get back together with him?"

The question caught Harper off guard. "Why would you ask that?"

Clearly uncomfortable, Molly shifted from one foot to the other and held out her hands. "I don't know. You were with him when you were my age. Then he died — or you thought he died — and I couldn't help but wonder if he was the great love of your life or something. I always assumed that was Jared, but then I heard the full story about what happened to Quinn and I wasn't sure. You never really talked about him, and I figured there had to be a reason for that."

"I didn't talk about Quinn because there was nothing left to say,"

Harper supplied. "I was young when I was with him. My relationship with Quinn was much different from my relationship with Jared. I was having fun back then."

"And you're not having fun now?"

"We're having a lot of fun. It's just a different type of fun. Jared and I were adults when we met, and not just in name only. Neither of us were looking for a relationship, but we found one anyway. It was more than either of us expected — so much more — and we blossomed together."

"Oh, that's so romantic." Molly took on a faraway expression. "You blossomed together. I'm going to ask Eric if he wants to blossom with me."

Harper recognized Molly's moony expression and made a tsking sound with her tongue. "Don't do that. It's no wonder Eric things you're a bit daft. You keep pushing the romance book angle on him. Life is not a chick flick. A real relationship means grappling with real feelings and emotions."

Molly balked. "And you don't think that Eric and I have a real relationship?"

"Of course I do. I even get that you're prone to fits of whimsy because of your age. You can't let that overtake the relationship, though."

"Is that what happened with Quinn?"

Harper was uncomfortable with the question. "No. I was young and having a good time. I wasn't worried about forever. Heck, I was barely worried about next week. Zander and I hadn't even really started GHI yet. I was floating and having a good time. It wasn't love, though."

"It wasn't?" Molly widened her eyes to comical proportions. "Oh, man. You're totally ruining my daydream. Are you saying you didn't love the guy who lost his memory and somehow magically made it back to you after years of suffering? That's so disappointing."

Harper bit back a chuckle. "I cared about him. I didn't love him, though. Of course, back then, I might have convinced myself that I did love him. It's all a little fuzzy now. What's important is that I didn't love him. Now that I've found Jared, I know what real love is. What I had with Quinn wasn't real."

"So ... what's going to happen now?" Molly was genuinely curious. "Will you just wave goodbye and never see him again? That seems anticlimactic. Like ... that's not how the movie is supposed to end."

"Life isn't a movie."

"No, but ... that doesn't feel like the right ending to me."

"No offense, Molly, but I'm not worried about the ending *you* want." Harper kept her tone stern. She was starting to regret bringing the enthusiastic younger woman out to the scene with her. The last thing she needed was relationship advice from a woman who tried to make her boyfriend dress up in a couple's costume on their first Halloween together. "I know the ending that's right for me, and Quinn isn't going to be there when it's time to cross the finish line. Jared is."

"I think you're taking this the wrong way," Molly protested. "I like Jared. In fact, I love him. If he hadn't seen you first and fallen head over heels, I totally would've gone after him."

"So, what's the problem?"

"The problem is that Quinn's story is more entertaining. That's the story that would win an Oscar."

"I don't care about his story, or if it would win awards," Harper said. "I care about the truth. That's the most important thing to me."

"I guess." Molly couldn't hide her disappointment. "I still like the other story better."

"And I happen to be with the blonde," a voice said from their left, causing both women to jerk and snap their heads in that direction as they registered a new player in the game. It was one they weren't expecting. "She's right. The truth is better than fiction every time."

EIGHTEEN

It was the man from the grocery store, the one Zander was convinced was checking him out (something Shawn played into, but Harper could tell he didn't believe). He stood at the edge of the dead cornstalks and stared at Molly and Harper, his hands clutched into fists at his sides.

Instinctively, Harper extended her arm to push Molly behind her and serve as a shield. Since she was young and foolish, though, Molly had other ideas.

"Who are you?"

The man's gaze bounced between Harper and Molly.

"Who are you?" He finally asked with a raspy voice, one that sounded as if his vocal cords had been raked over barbed wire at some point over the course of his life.

"I'm Molly Parker." The younger woman was all business as she planted her hands on her hips. "May we ask what you're doing in this particular cornfield? It's kind of late in the season for shucking."

Even though she was annoyed, Harper couldn't stop herself from being impressed with Molly's moxie. The woman was so self-possessed that she simply refused to believe anything bad could happen to her ... even though bad things had already happened to her.

The stranger snagged Harper's gaze and extended a finger. "Is she for real?"

Nervous, Harper licked her lips and nodded. "She is. She's also out of the loop. She doesn't recognize you."

"And you do?" He cocked a challenging eyebrow, as if daring Harper to wow him with knowledge she didn't have.

"I don't know your name," Harper clarified. "I've seen you around, though. You were in the grocery store yesterday."

"Oh." Molly made a clucking sound with her tongue as she bobbed her head. "Is this the guy that's hot for Zander's body?"

"I most certainly am not!" The man barked, his eyes flashing. "Is she saying what I think she's saying?"

Harper held her hands up in a placating manner. "Don't get worked up about it. Zander thinks everyone wants him, including every Kardashian he sees on the television. He simply likes to talk. There's no reason to freak out."

"Who says I'm freaking out?" A muscle worked in the man's jaw as he looked Harper from top to bottom. "How would you like it if I made you uncomfortable and said I was watching you in the grocery store?"

"I think we're well beyond that," Harper said. "You obviously followed us out here, which is creepy, and I already feel uncomfortable. What is it that you want? Why have you been following me?"

"Believe it or not, I'm not following you," the man shot back. "Er, well, I guess I kind of am. I'm not following you for the reasons you think, though, and I wanted you to come out here anyway. It was fate ... or something like it."

Harper had trouble following the conversation. "I'm sorry but ... I don't understand." She felt lost, awash in confusion. She was also worried. No matter what Jared said, Harper felt in her heart that Quinn couldn't be a murderer. That meant this guy, whoever he was, had to be the culprit.

That put Harper and Molly in a very precarious position.

The look the man pinned her with was searching, as if he was looking for the lie he was certain she was hiding. Finally, he merely shook his head. "You really don't know, do you? I thought for sure all that was a smokescreen. I figured Jackson had to tell you what he was up to. Isn't that why you're out here?"

Harper's heart jolted at the mention of Quinn's last name. "I'm out here because the woman who owns the property thinks the scarecrow is possessed."

The man widened his eyes to comic proportions as he took in the staked figure behind Molly. "She thinks that thing is coming to life and wandering around? That's the stupidest thing I've ever heard."

Offended on Betty's behalf, Harper squared her shoulders and smoothed the front of her T-shirt. "I don't like your tone. As for Betty, I've never known her to be crazy. That means she saw something out here. Why do you think we're hanging in a barren cornfield the day before Thanksgiving?"

"I thought you were out here looking for the stash."

"The stash of what?"

"My stash!" The man thumped his chest in frustration as his gaze prowled the ground near the scarecrow. "It was years ago, but it has to be close. I know it. If I could just remember, I would be able to find it and get out of here."

"Find what?"

"Happily ever after. That's what I'm looking for, and I'm not leaving until I find it."

"HERE WE GO."

Mel furrowed his brow as he gazed at his computer screen.

"What have you got?" Jared asked, turning his eyes to his partner. "Have you got more on Quinn?"

"I've got a match for the guy in the grocery store," Mel replied, contemplative. "It's ... weird."

"I'm going to need more than that," Jared prodded, his patience wearing thin.

"His name is David Harding. He was big news around these parts about six years ago. I can't believe I forgot his face. It was splashed around every news station in the area for three days because there was a manhunt."

"There was a manhunt for that guy?" Mel officially had Jared's attention, so the younger man rolled his desk chair closer to his partner's work space. "What did he do? Wait ... was he a murderer? I don't like the idea that he was watching Zander and Harper in the store if that's the case."

"Not a murderer," Mel clarified, shaking his head. "He was a bank robber. He and two other people — a man and a woman — managed to get away with more than a million dollars after an armed robbery at a Comerica branch almost six years ago."

"He just wandered in with a gun and held them up? That was stupid."

"He wore a mask." Mel took on a far-off look that told Jared he was searching his memory. "He wore a mask and threatened to kill everyone in the bank. He didn't pull the trigger, but the security guard was worried enough about his mental stability that he thought there was a good chance Harding would lose it and start shooting everyone on the premises. Thankfully that didn't occur, which was a relief, but it was a huge deal at the time because the FBI believed there was an inside man involved in that caper."

"If Harding was so easily identified, that must've meant he was caught relatively quickly."

"He was. He was taken into custody in St. Clair. He was trying to hide in a cabin by the lake, but it belonged to an uncle and he wasn't hard to track down. He didn't have the money on him when it happened, though, which made it difficult to press charges."

"Wait ... ." Jared held up his hand to slow the story. "How was Harding identified? Security footage?"

"Kind of, but not like you think." Mel rubbed the back of his neck as he tried to remember the story in the correct order. "All three individuals wore all black, including ski masks. It was obvious one of them was a woman. The other two were men.

"When they fled, they were parked several blocks over," he continued. "It was a stolen car that they abandoned within twenty minutes of fleeing. Unfortunately for them, Harding took off his mask when they were dumping the car and there happened to be a camera across the road. The other two individuals were never seen on camera, but Harding was identified through a screenshot."

Jared made a face. "That doesn't sound smart."

"He was not the smartest cookie in the box," Mel confirmed. "He was easy to track down, and the FBI had his face plastered all over the television stations. Technically, we weren't involved. Still, there was a chance he might be hiding in Whisper Cove, so I coordinated with the local bureau officials. I remember there was even a sighting of Harding, out by the old Miller place. It turned out to be rubbish, though, and he was caught in St. Clair."

"What about his partners?"

"They were never caught," Mel replied. "He refused to roll over on them. Was even a little smug in court, if I remember the footage from the television correctly. They couldn't actually nail him for the robbery in the end because they couldn't find the money. He got in trouble for stealing the car and that was it. He got sent away for five years."

"And now he's out and back," Jared noted.

"And hanging around Whisper Cove." Mel's mind was working fast and furious. "I can't help but wonder if that's because he really was in town six years ago and that wasn't a false sighting."

"I'm more interested in Judy Lange," Jared argued. "This guy was at the hospital the night she was killed. To my knowledge, Judy Lange was not in town six years ago."

"She might make sense as the accomplice, though," Mel pointed out. "We know a woman was with him. Maybe it was Judy."

Jared pressed his hand to his forehead as he considered the idea. "How can we prove that she was here at the time of the bank robbery?"

"I think we start with her mother."

"I can't think of another place to start," Jared agreed grimly. "Let's do it."

. . .

"YOU'RE LOOKING FOR happily ever after?" Harper was convinced the man was crazy ... or maybe a little delusional. She could think of no other reason for his outlandish statement. "Do you want us to leave you alone with the scarecrow so you can find it?"

"Oh, you're so funny," the man drawled, rolling his eyes. "The scarecrow isn't part of the happily ever after. The money is."

"What money?"

"Um ... the bank robbery money." He said it in such a manner that Harper felt a bit silly for asking the question. "I hid it here six years ago, but I can't remember exactly where. They've changed some of the landmarks."

It took Harper what felt like forever to catch up with the conversation. "Wait ... you robbed a bank six years ago and hid the money out here?"

"Ding! Ding! Ding! We have a winner!" He jabbed his finger in the air and did a little dance. "That didn't take too long. Oh, wait, it took forever. It's no wonder that people think blondes are stupid. You're about as dumb as they come."

Molly, who had been listening with rapt attention, found her voice. "Don't talk to my friend that way," she snapped, her tone laden with annoyance. "You don't even know Harper. She's one of the smartest people I know."

"If she was smart, she wouldn't have allowed Jackson back into her life."

After the man's second reference to her former boyfriend, Harper couldn't refrain from asking the obvious question. "How do you know Quinn?"

"Oh, Quinn and I go way back. We're the best of friends. I think we're going to head to the bar later tonight and have drinks while reminiscing about old times and the fact that he screwed me over. Like ... big time."

Harper struggled to keep her cool. Even though the man didn't look armed, that didn't mean he wasn't dangerous. He'd just owned up to being a bank robber, after all. He was seen heading into the hospital the night Judy Lange died. He could very well be a murderer

"I think we should start from the beginning," Harper prodded gently. "I desperately want to help you here, but I am having difficulty following the conversation."

"That's because you're blond."

Harper barely managed to bite back the insult on the tip of her tongue. "Yes, well, perhaps I'll dye my hair when I get home. I hear brunettes have more fun. Anyway, I need more information if I'm going to help. My understanding is that you robbed a bank. Are you talking about that big Comerica heist six years ago?"

"That would be the one. We got away with a million dollars because they had overflow in the vault. We knew they would because Jackson was working the books for them, and he was the one who figured out there was a big score right under our fingertips. We got away with it and everything ... and then I lost it."

Harper's heart gave a jolt at the words. "Are you saying that Quinn robbed the bank with you?" The idea was preposterous. And yet, in the back of her mind, part of Harper believed the charge. The accusation made sense.

"Of course he helped rob the bank," he shot back. "He was the one who came up with the idea."

"He did." Harper felt numb. "Harding. Your name is David Harding, right? I remember from the newscasts back then. I should've recognized your face."

Impressed, Harding puffed out his chest. "That's me. It's good to be famous."

"Yes, well ... it's good to be a lot of things." She risked a glance at Molly and found the younger woman watching the scene with unveiled interest ... and a small bit of terror. "How do you and Quinn even know each other?"

"We met when we were in school," Harding replied, his gaze back on the ground as he searched for ... something. Harper had no idea what he was looking for, but apparently he stole a million dollars from the bank and hid it in a field. That meant he was probably looking for a bag or something. Burying a bag in the middle of nowhere didn't seem like a good idea to her, but she was hardly in a position to argue with a potentially crazy man. "I was a student at CMU. He was at Northwood. He wanted to have some fun one night and we ended up at the same bar ... it was kind of a friendship for the ages, if you know what I mean."

"I have no idea what you mean."

"We were opposites but best friends," Harding explained. "He was the thinker, and I was the doer. It was the perfect partnership."

Harper felt sick to her stomach. "You guys worked together more than once, didn't you? You did multiple jobs together."

"Only one bank job," Harding clarified. "We bounced around from idea to idea, trying to find a big one to stick. He was intent on breaking into the bigger real estate racket — he had a plan for Whisper Cove, in fact — but it wasn't easy, and Judy kept screwing up to the point where I thought for sure he was going to kill her if she lost the money we needed one more time."

Harper's heart skipped a beat. "Judy Lange?"

"Yeah."

"You guys worked with Judy Lange?"

"I believe that's what I said."

Harper was officially dumbfounded. "I don't understand."

"That seems to be the perpetual state for you," Harding said. "I don't think it's important that you understand. What's important is that we find my money. I need to get out of this stupid town, but I'm not going without my money."

Harper wanted to press him further, but her mind was working at a fantastic rate. She couldn't think of the next question. Luckily, Molly didn't have that problem.

"How did the money end up in this field?" Molly asked. "I mean ... I don't get it. Why would you rob a bank and then hide the money? Isn't the point to spend the money?"

"Of course that's the point." Harding shot Molly a "well, duh" look and grimaced. "We were under the gun, though. Jackson couldn't take the money home because he had a girlfriend who might stumble over it — good old Blondie here — and no one trusted Judy with the money. I was supposed to hang onto it until we could all rendezvous and then take off. I heard the cops were closing in, though, because they caught me on a camera. I knew I was in trouble."

"You knew you were in trouble?" Molly cocked her head. "Oh, I think I get it." She brightened considerably. "You hid the money because you didn't want to leave it with Quinn and Judy. You knew they would spend it while you were in prison — and you were pretty sure you were going to prison — so you buried the money in a spot where you could claim it years later and cut them out of the job entirely."

Harding's grin was lightning quick and almost charming. "I like you. You're much smarter than the blonde."

Molly basked in the compliment. "Oh, well, thank you."

"Yes, she's an absolute delight," Harper interjected, something occurring to her. "If you went to jail, why not cut a deal and roll over on Quinn and Judy? You might have gotten off with zero time behind bars."

"That's true, and I considered that." Harding sobered. "The thing is, I had a million dollars and I was the only one who knew where it was. If I turned in my friends, the cops would've made me return the money as part of any deal. I didn't want that. Besides, they ultimately couldn't pin the robbery on me, just the car theft."

"I remember that," Harper mused. "People were upset but there was nothing they could do."

"No. I would rather lose five years of my life to prison — which wasn't really that bad — than lose a million dollars. I decided to bide my time."

"Right." Harper's mind was working a mile a minute. "Were you in touch with Quinn during your prison stay? He couldn't have been happy about you keeping that money from him."

"He had a hundred grand. I think that's what he used when he ran. He might've even taken Judy's hundred grand, because that's his way. I didn't expect to see him again. Sure enough, though, he made a big splash coming back at the same time I got out of prison. That can't possibly be a coincidence."

"No," Harper agreed. "Not a coincidence."

"Definitely not," Quinn agreed, taking everyone by surprise as he walked into the field and raised a gun. He seemingly appeared out of nowhere.

Harper felt as if she was trapped in quicksand as she tried to grasp what was happening. Harding's eyes went wide as he reached toward his hip, perhaps searching for a weapon. Molly whimpered and turned on her heel, fleeing into the field. Harper remained rooted to her spot, dumbfounded disbelief washing over her as the man she thought she knew leveled a weapon on his former friend ... and then coldheartedly pulled the trigger without a second thought.

"You've had that coming for a long time, David. I'm glad to be the one to deliver it."

NINETEEN

T he blood was roaring in Harper's ears as she tried to make sense of the scene in front of her. Harding hit the ground with a sickening thud, his eyes open and unseeing. It was obvious he was dead.

Quinn didn't seem bothered by that in the slightest as he turned his full attention to Harper, ignoring the dead man on the ground, and focusing on the woman he briefly shared a life with. "That's better, huh? He always was an idiot. Now we can talk without him interrupting. There's nothing I hate more than interruptions."

Harper tried to form words but came up empty.

"Where did your little friend go?" Quinn narrowed his eyes as he searched the field. "She couldn't have gone far. Should we look for her?" He held out his hand as if it were the most normal thing in the world, as if he actually expected Harper to take it and go on her merry way with him.

His reaction was enough to loosen Harper's tongue. "Leave her alone." Her tone was chilling. "She has nothing to do with this. Leave her be."

"I don't think I can really do that, Harper." Quinn sounded so reasonable, so much like the man she remembered, Harper half expected to bolt to a sitting position in her bed because this was surely nothing more than a bad dream. "She witnessed a murder. Personally, I think it was retribution, but that's not how she's going to spin it to the cops ... and I already have enough strikes against me as far as the locals are concerned."

"Leave her alone," Harper repeated, fury taking the place of shock as she fought to control her emotions. "She has nothing to do with this."

"If you wanted things to be like that, you should've left her out of this."

"I didn't realize you would be killing people in a cornfield. I'll know better next time."

"I bet you will." Quinn let loose a wink that made Harper's blood run cold. "I'm sure you have a lot of questions. I don't really have time to answer them, though. I need to find the money that David hid out here ... and then I need to be hitting the road. If you're a good girl, I'll take you with me."

"I think I'll pass."

"I don't think I'm going to give you that option." Quinn was matter-of-fact as he shoved the gun into the waistband of his jeans and leaned over to search David's body. "I'm going to assume he couldn't remember where he buried my money and that's why he's been in this field every day for the past week. He came straight here after being released from prison. I knew he would."

Harper wet her dry lips and worked overtime to tamp down her growing panic. "I don't understand. How did you pull this off? We were together back then. You weren't a bank robber. I would've known."

"We only robbed one bank."

"Still ... I would've known."

"Oh, Harper, don't be too hard on yourself." Quinn sounded as if he was talking to a young child rather than his former girlfriend. "I worked hard to keep you from knowing what I was up to. Of course, you made it easy. You were always so wrapped up with Zander and your ghosts that you made the perfect cover without even realizing it.

"I mean, who would suspect Quinn Jackson, the young man who had everything going for him?" he continued. "He had a beautiful girl-friend and a great job at the bank. He had no reason to steal. You saw what I wanted you to see. Nothing more."

Things slipped into place for Harper. "You were the inside man for the bank job. I remember hearing Mel talk about it over dinner one night. He said the Feds assumed there was an inside man."

"And even after David went to prison they wouldn't let it go. They were always sniffing around. I have no idea if they suspected me, but I needed to get the heat off. That's why I decided to fake my own death and get out of this town."

Even though she'd just watched him kill a man, Harper couldn't help being disheartened by the words. "You faked your death?"

"Of course I did. You didn't believe that whole amnesia story, did you? I faked my death and escaped to a new life. There was nothing holding me here. I knew there was no way David would tell me where he hid the money, so I had to wait until he was released from prison.

"I headed to New York because I figured it would be an easy city to disappear in, and I was right," he continued. "Making a buck in New York is much easier than in Michigan. I don't think it's because the people are more intelligent or anything, mind you, but there are simply more people to con.

"I planned on catching David the minute they let him out of prison, taking him hostage until he gave me my money," he said. "It didn't quite work out that way, though. They released him a full week early, so I was behind.

"I didn't want to disrupt your life, if that's any consolation," he said. "I had no interest in seeing you at all. Then I found out Judy was in town. I thought she was long gone, although it made sense she would come back because she wanted her cut, too."

"It wasn't an accident that she had an accident in the same spot you did," Harper mused. "You caused it."

"I did." Quinn was blasé, unbothered by his murderous tendencies. "I ran her off the road. She didn't die, though. I was smart enough to check, but she saw me and called for help right away. I think she fudged the timeline to the cops, though, which put me in a bind. I had no choice but to retreat.

"I thought the paramedics would release her, but she allowed them to transport her to the hospital," he continued. "That was on purpose. She thought the hospital staff could protect her. I was worried when I saw David in the parking lot, knew I was working on a truncated timetable. If they decided to work together, I would be at a disadvantage, and I didn't want that.

"I still thought I could get into town without running into anyone I knew way back when until I followed David the next day and he came here," he said. "I was going to confront him, demand my money right here, and end it all ... but then a car showed up and out popped you and Zander. David hid right away; I lost him. You screwed up my plans, which meant I had no choice but to go public."

Harper was flabbergasted. "You didn't even want to see me at all."

"You seem surprised. I have fond memories of you — you were so adorable and sweet — but I was hardly in love with you. Still, you have certain ... charms. You also have access to the police, something I figured out quickly when I got back. I needed to know if they knew anything about David, so I showed myself to you ... and then kept coming around."

Harper felt like an absolute idiot. "And here I thought you were trying to make a connection."

"Not to belabor the point or anything, but you create these problems yourself," Quinn argued. "You want to see the best in everybody. Nobody can live up to your expectations."

"Jared can."

"Yes, well, Jared is a modern marvel, isn't he?" Quinn sneered. "That guy has been all up in my business. I thought he was going to be another country bumpkin police officer, but he's been watching me far too closely. He stopped by again yesterday to warn me that if I hurt you he would hurt me. Oh, he didn't say it in so many words, but the message was clear. I wanted to punch him in the face, but that would've broken my cover."

"And landed you in jail ... or the hospital."

"You have a lot of faith in him." Quinn's smirk was evil. "You haven't learned a thing since we were together, have you? People aren't meant to mate for life, Harper. Nothing is forever."

"Some things are forever," Harper argued. "I don't really care about your assessment of my private life, though. It doesn't involve you. I want to know what your plan is here."

"I'm going to find my money."

"Yes, I get that," she said dryly. "The problem is, you've killed the only man who knows where the money is. How do you expect to get your answers without David leading the way?"

"That's where you come in."

Harper stiffened. "Me? I don't know where your money is."

"No, but you see ghosts." Quinn sounded rational, but his eyes flashed with what Harper could only describe as rampant insanity. "I want you to talk to David's ghost and find out where the money is. There's no reason for him to keep the information to himself any longer. He's dead and can't spend the money. It's all mine."

Harper worked her jaw, unsure what to say. Finally, she went with the truth. "It doesn't work that way. David isn't a ghost."

"Sure he is. You told me that those who die traumatic deaths come back as ghosts. David died a traumatic death. Get answers from him. I don't have all day."

Harper didn't consider herself a violent person, but she recognized she could kill Quinn without any qualms if the opportunity arose. "Even if he is a ghost, it takes time for them to come back. They don't immediately pop into existence."

"Well, you'd better make him pop into existence. I am out of patience with this stupid town and you, for that matter. Enough is enough. Find my money. If you don't, you're going to be joining David. That's your motivation. Hop to it."

WELL, THAT WAS A waste of time," Mel lamented as he and Jared left the home where Patty Lange lived a second time. "She honestly has no idea who her daughter hung around with or what she might've been involved in before leaving the area."

"No," Jared agreed, his expression thoughtful as he climbed into the passenger seat of Mel's cruiser. "She did say that Judy absolutely could've returned to town and she wouldn't have known about it. I don't know how else to pin down Judy's movements. She could've been working under any number of aliases."

"That's true." Mel rubbed his chin as he stared through the windshield. "If we're working under the assumption that Judy was the female accomplice — and that seems to make the most sense — then that means we only have to figure out the male accomplice."

"Yeah, well, that's easier said than done." Jared frowned when his phone started ringing. "Hold on. I don't recognize this number. It's probably a telemarketer. Hello?"

Mildly curious, Mel watched the color drain from his partner's face as he listened to whoever talked on the other end of the phone. Jared was intense when he started talking.

"You stay right there, Molly," he ordered, jabbing his finger at the ignition so Mel knew to start the car. "We're on our way. Don't do anything to draw attention to yourself ... and that includes going after Harper. We're on our way. I'll get Harper. Do you understand?" He waited for an answer. "Good. We're five minutes out. We'll be there before you know it."

He was grim when he disconnected the call and stared out the window. "You need to go to the cornfield by Betty Miller's house. Harper is there ... and she's in trouble."

"What kind of trouble?"

"The kind that answers all of our questions," Jared replied, his stomach twisting as he thought about Harper's heart-shaped face and blue eyes. "Go fast. Quinn has Harper, and he'll kill her if she doesn't produce what he's looking for. I have no doubt about that."

"We're going." Mel's knuckles were white he gripped the steering wheel. "Was Quinn the third partner?"

"That's my guess."

"It makes sense."

"Too bad we didn't put it together sooner."

"I DON'T KNOW WHAT you want me to do."

Harper was frustrated and near tears as she stomped through the cornfield, Quinn directly on her heels.

"I want you to find my money," Quinn growled, his patience wearing thin. "How many different times do I have to tell you this? That's my money. I worked hard for it. I want it."

"And yet I don't know where it is." In her head, Harper knew she should delay Quinn until help could arrive. There was every reason to hope Molly managed to escape and call for help. In her gut, though, Harper was dealing with a huge mound of fury that refused to dissipate. She was frustrated, and there was only one person to take it out on.

"You know what? I am really angry with you." She took Quinn by surprise when she spun to face him, her eyes flashing with anger. "Do you have any idea how I felt when I thought you died in the woods? I kept picturing you cold and shivering with a mortal wound. Instead you were already out of the state and living it up in New York. You're a truly awful individual."

"Oh, don't be that way." Quinn made a face. "You were the one thing I didn't want to leave. Honestly, I wasn't lying about you being adorable. I enjoyed the time we spent together. I would've enjoyed it more without Zander always hanging around, but I had plans for him. He was going to meet an untimely end as soon as I could work out a believable accident."

Harper's blood ran cold. "Oh, well, you're such a prince."

"Don't take that tone with me." Quinn was deathly serious. "I deserve some respect. I know you loved me and your heart was broken when you thought I died, but I had to get out of this place. I would've gone to prison otherwise."

"How did you even do it?" Harper pressed. "Your blood was found at the scene. There was enough blood that everyone believed you couldn't survive."

"That was on purpose. I banked some blood, had it refrigerated, and then used it after I staged the car. It wasn't difficult."

"You banked blood?" Harper was horrified. "That is ... disgusting."

"And it worked like a charm," Quinn shot back. "After the initial search — and you're right, I was already gone by the time they even started looking — no one was searching for me. I could have a regular life and that's what I wanted. Did I miss you? Not really. I missed the sex and you were a lot of fun. It's not as if I was a monk, though. There have been plenty of other women since you."

"You are a true joy," Harper drawled. "I mean ... a true prince in a sea of frogs."

Quinn winked. "I think so, too."

"There's only one problem with your little plan."

"Oh, yeah? What's that?"

"Jared knows you're up to something and he'll never stop hunting you. You might kill me — I know that's your plan — but Jared will make it his life's mission to hunt you down."

"Please." Quinn rolled his eyes, disdain evident. "He'll be so crushed he won't even be able to get out of bed. That guy is a total pansy. His whole life is about you. It's absolutely ridiculous the way he acts."

"That's how a real man acts," Harper muttered as she moved over a clump of fallen cornstalks. "He's the best man I've ever met. I didn't even know that men could be as good as him until we got together. I thought all relationships were supposed to be boring and ho-hum before him because that's what I learned from you." She paused and gave him a saucy look. "By the way, I never loved you. Not even a little."

"Oh, you're making that up to save face. I happen to know that you searched for me for a year. People all over town have told me that."

"I searched for you out of guilt," Harper countered. "I felt bad that you stayed in Whisper Cove when you had a chance to leave. I understood you hated it here. I should've let you go. I thought you stayed because of me. I get I was wrong about that, but the reason I searched for so long was because I felt guilty. I thought you wouldn't have died if I told you to go."

"That's not very convincing."

"Well, it's the truth. In fact ... ." Harper didn't get a chance to finish because all the air whooshed out of her lungs as a set of hands reached out of the thick clump of cornstalks to her right.

"What the ... ?" Quinn was shocked, incensed, when he realized they weren't alone. The fact that Harper practically disappeared in front of his eyes was enough to jolt his system and had him grappling for his gun. "Is that little Molly coming back to play?"

"Not quite," a dark voice said, moving behind Quinn as the unmistakable sound of the hammer being pulled back on a firearm filled the air. "I thought you would rather play with me instead."

Quinn froze with his hand on the gun, which remained in his waistband. He recognized Jared's voice, and it was the last thing he wanted to hear. He also understood the cop meant business, and that probably wouldn't bode well for him.

"What are you doing here, Detective Monroe? I think you've got the wrong idea."

"No, I don't. Now take your hands off that gun or I will blow your head off. I won't even think twice about doing it."

Harper poked her head out of the cornstalks even though Mel tried to drag her away from the scene. She couldn't look away. The expression on Jared's face was chilling, but she'd never been so happy to see anyone in her entire life.

"I don't know that I think that's in my best interests," Quinn hedged. "I don't think I'm built for prison, so maybe I should force you to take me out."

"If that's your decision, I'm happy to oblige you."

It was a dare of sorts. Quinn knew that. When he met Harper's serious gaze, he realized she knew it, too. She believed without a shadow of a doubt that Jared would kill him. Even though he wasn't keen on going to prison, Quinn valued his own neck too much to risk it.

He pulled his hands away from the gun and held them up,

defeated. "Fine. I just want you to know, though, I blame all of this on David. He fouled things up from the beginning. It was the perfect plan otherwise."

"Yeah, the perfect plan," Jared agreed as he confiscated Quinn's gun. "Two people are dead. That doesn't sound like the perfect plan to me."

"I guess it depends on which way you look at it. On what's important to you."

Jared's eyes snagged with Harper's, warmth washing over him at the sight of her smile. "I guess it does depend on what's important to you. The sad thing is, you never had the appropriate priorities from the start."

"If you say so."

"I *know* so."

TWENTY

Zander and Shawn were pacing the house when Jared and Harper arrived. They heard the bulk of the tale through the grapevine — a panicked Eric melting down thanks to a phone call from Molly — but Zander refused to relax until he saw Harper with his own eyes.

"Harper!" He jerked his best friend into a smothering hug as Jared shut the door. "I was so worried. I can't believe I didn't go with you today. I'm so sorry."

Harper patted his back before extricating herself from the painful embrace. "I'm okay. I'm not hurt or anything. David Harding is another story."

"Good." Zander smoothed Harper's messy hair. "Now I can say 'I told you so' without feeling guilty."

Even though she'd been through the wringer, Harper couldn't hold back her chuckle. "I guess you've earned that."

"No, he hasn't," Jared countered, leading Harper to the couch so she could sit. He removed her shoes himself, shooting Zander a warning look before settling beside her. "I don't think that's necessary."

"Hey, I've been suspicious of that guy since I met him," Zander argued, slapping at Shawn's hand when he tried to draw Zander away from the couch. Instead, Zander flopped into the spot on the other side of Harper and grabbed her hand. "People should listen to me more often."

"Yes, we all agree that you're a genius," Jared drawled, dragging a restless hand through his hair. "We'll throw you a party tomorrow, okay? For the rest of the day, let's table the crowing."

"I think that's a good idea," Shawn agreed, his eyes on Harper's pale face. "Are you sure you're okay, Harper? No offense, but you don't look so good."

Harper offered him a rueful smile. "It's been a long day."

"We heard most of it," Shawn supplied. "We know that Quinn was working with the other guy, the one from the store, but we're not sure how it all overlaps."

"It's kind of convoluted," Jared admitted. "Basically, Quinn was always a scammer of sorts, looking for a quick way to make a buck. He met up with David Harding in college and they worked a few jobs together. When Quinn got the job at the bank, he realized they could get their hands on a lot of money. They needed a third person and David knew Judy, someone both men thought they could control, so that's how they ended up working together.

"They each took a hundred grand after the robbery, and David was supposed to hide the rest until they could dole it out," he continued. "David figured out the cops were after him, though, and buried the money in Betty Miller's cornfield. He thought it would be better that way in case the cops caught up with him because he couldn't lie and say he wasn't involved if they found the cash."

"I'm guessing Quinn didn't like that," Shawn noted.

"No, but there was nothing he could do about it," Jared said. "David was caught and locked away, but all they could truly get him for was auto theft. Quinn's problem was that the Feds were convinced the robbery was an inside job and that they would look to him eventually. He couldn't run without creating a manhunt situation, so he faked his death."

"Why come back now?" Zander asked, legitimately curious. "Why wait all this time?"

"Because David got out of prison about a week and a half ago," Jared replied. "His release was early. Apparently Quinn had a different plan, but it was thrown out the door when David was released. Unfortunately for David, the field was planted differently since his last visit and he couldn't remember where he buried the money."

"That's a total bummer, huh?" Shawn smirked.

"He was out there digging a bunch of holes looking for the money, which explains why Betty was convinced the scarecrow was alive," Jared explained. "She kept seeing movement. It was David, not the scarecrow. I have no proof of this, but I'm going to guess David is the one who pretended to make the scarecrow talk to scare her away. Betty claims otherwise, that the scarecrow was doing it, but that's the only thing that makes sense to me."

"What was Quinn's plan? I mean ... my understanding is that he killed David. How did he think he would find the money without him?"

Harper stirred. "That's where I came in. He thought David's ghost would tell me where the money was so he could simply dig it up and be on his merry way."

"What was he going to do with you?" Zander asked.

"He said I could go with him, but we all know that's not what he had planned. If I found the money, he would've killed me. Even if I didn't find the money, he would've done the same. He had no problem killing David. He didn't even blink when he did it. It was ... nothing to him. I was nothing to him either."

"Heart, you can't get yourself worked up about this." Jared snagged her hand and pressed it to his chest. "He was a sociopath. You couldn't have known."

"Really?" Harper wasn't convinced. "I was with him for a decent amount of time. It seems to me that's something I should've picked up on."

"I think you did pick up on it. You simply didn't realize it. You said it yourself, you were young. You didn't want to see evil in the world, so you simply looked the other way. There's nothing wrong with that."

It didn't feel that way to Harper. "I still think I should've known."

"You can't go back and change things." Jared's fingers were gentle when they shifted a strand of hair behind her ear. "The most important thing is that you're okay. You have no idea the terror I felt when Molly called to tell me what was going on. I was sure I would get there too late, and the thought wrecked me."

Harper managed a small smile. "You came through. At first, I was freaked out when Mel grabbed me and dragged me into the stalks. Then I saw you and knew everything would be okay."

"All I could think about was getting to you. It took every ounce of self-restraint I have not to race across the field and kill Quinn with my bare hands. That walk through the stalks was the longest of my life."

"Well, it's over now."

"It definitely is." Jared wrapped his arms around Harper and held her tight as she curled into him. He could read the exhaustion on her face. She needed quiet time to think and decompress. He would have to force Zander into taking a step back to make sure it happened, but he was prepared and ready when the right moment showed itself.

"What about Molly?" Shawn asked, clearly trying to change the subject. "Is she okay?"

"Molly bolted into the stalks the second Quinn appeared," Jared answered. "She reacted out of instinct and is feeling guilty for leaving Harper."

"That's stupid," Harper muttered. "She did the exact right thing."

"Which is what I told her. She'll be fine once she rests for a bit. I think the same can be said for you."

Harper lifted her chin and met his eyes. "Yeah. I'm tired. I'm also cold. I think I'm going to hit the bathroom and take a long bath. I mean ... if you don't mind."

"I don't mind. I think it's a good idea." Jared gave her a soft kiss, one that promised a myriad of things with one gentle touch. "How about I order some Chinese food and we eat in bed tonight, huh? How does that sound?"

"That sounds like something I'm not invited to," Zander groused.

Jared ignored him when Harper nodded in gratitude. "Good. I'll place the order. By the time you're done in the bathtub, the food will be here. I figure we can watch some television and shut out the rest of the world."

"That's a good plan."

Jared waited until Harper shut her bedroom door before speaking again. "Zander, we need to talk."

For his part, Zander was expecting Jared to start barking orders. That didn't stop him from making a pinched face. "Oh, I hate it when you use that tone."

"I know you do." Jared was calm but refused to back down. "I want you to leave Harper alone for the rest of the night. Tomorrow morning, though, I'm going to temporarily suspend my rule about you climbing into bed with us. I think that will make Harper feel better. I want you to wait until after nine, though. Everyone has the day off and I want to sleep in."

Zander was instantly suspicious. "You're inviting me into bed with you?"

"There's no need to make it sound dirty."

"I'm simply asking for clarification."

"I want you to make Harper laugh," Jared corrected. "She's not ready for it yet. She will be tomorrow. You're the best man for the job."

Zander puffed out his chest. "That could be said about almost anything."

"Yes, well, I'll keep that in mind."

"What about Quinn?" Shawn asked. "What's going to happen to him?"

"He's in our jail until Friday. Then he'll be transferred to a federal facility. I believe he has a lot of questions to answer."

"Will Harper have to testify?"

"Probably. I expect the national news media will be all over this place once the story breaks, too. It's too big not to draw a lot of attention."

"We're not going to be able to shield Harper from that," Zander noted, serious. "She won't be able to get away from people wanting to interview her. She won't like that."

"We'll do what we can to protect her, but I'm not sure how that's going to work either," Jared admitted. "We have a few days to make a plan. This won't break until Friday. That's good for us."

"Yeah." Zander narrowed his eyes as he studied the police officer. "What about you? How are you feeling?"

"Thankful. I thought I might lose her."

"Some things are meant to be," Zander countered. "You and Harper are meant to be."

"I think that's the nicest thing you've ever said to me."

"Yeah, well, you saved my best friend. You've earned it."

"Yeah." Jared exhaled heavily and rubbed his forehead. "While I have you in a magnanimous mood, there's something else I want to tell you."

"What?"

"I'm proposing to Harper over Christmas."

Whatever he was expecting, that wasn't it. Zander jerked up his chin. "What?"

"Don't act so surprised. You knew it was coming. We've talked about this before."

"Yes, but I didn't know it was happening this fast. Why now?"

"Because there's no reason to wait," Jared replied simply. "All I could think about during that drive to the field was how much I love her, how I can't live without her. Those feelings aren't going to change. Not a month from now ... or a year from now ... or a decade from now. She's it for me, and I want to make it official."

Instead of melting down like he expected, Jared was pleasantly surprised to see Zander fighting off tears. They were of the good variety, though, not the whiny.

"Are you okay with that?" Jared asked pointedly. "I want to make sure before I move forward. I would rather deal with meltdowns now instead of in the future."

"I guess that depends," Zander hedged, recovering quickly.

"On what?"

"If I can help you pick out Harper's ring."

Jared's lips curved up. In truth, he'd always wanted the persnickety man with him for that particular task. "Sure. As long as you promise not to give away my plan. I want to make it something special."

Zander mimed crossing his heart. "I promise. I would never ruin this for her. I love her, too."

"I know you do. That's why we're going to do this together."

"Cool." Zander shot Jared an enthusiastic thumbs-up. "By the way, you know I'm going to be obnoxious when it comes to finding the exact right ring, don't you?"

"I never doubted it."

"As long as you're aware."

Shawn snorted at the two men, amusement lighting his handsome features. "You guys are going to be a fearsome twosome going forward. I'm looking forward to watching it unfold."

"That makes two of us," Zander said, his eyes sparkling.

"Three," Jared corrected. "There are three of us in this, and we're going to make all of Harper's dreams come true. I'll settle for nothing less."

Made in United States
North Haven, CT
17 January 2024

47580589R00118